TALES
OF
BIZARRE
DETECTIVES

Russ Crossley

Published by 53rd Street Publishing
www.53rdstreetpublising.com

Introduction

Welcome to this first collection by two authors of fantastic fiction, R.G. Hart, and Russ Crossley. While these two authors normally write in different genres, Russ Hart paranormal romance, and Russ Crossley science fiction and fantasy, they both often write about interesting female protagonists in fantastic settings.

This is why 53rd Street Publishing decided to blend their short fiction into this anthology of six selected stories of bizarre detectives on strange cases. Between these pages you'll find detectives who time travel, detectives who aren't human, and a secret agent who must travel to another world to save this one.

We hope you'll find these Tales of Bizarre Detectives sometimes amusing, terrifying, and exciting as the heroes must fight seemingly impossible odds, and defeat seemingly invincible enemies to save the day for all human and non-human kind.

Table of Contents

Tales of Bizarre Detectives

R.G. Hart and Russ Crossley

Published by 53rd Street Publishing

ISBN 978-1-927621-04-2

Logo image by:

Engraver | Dreamstime.com

Big Hairy Deal

OR ONCE I WASN'T in the office when our future four-legged client bounded passed me snarling at screaming civilians. At the time I was concentrating on squeezing a grapefruit at Mo's Fruitland on Bleeker street, near the office.

My office is located on the third floor of a three-story, mold-covered brick walk-up above Bleeker Street in the city of Vancouver. And not the pretty-multi-cultural-Mecca-Vancouver by the sea you're thinking of--the one on the west coast of Canada. My Vancouver is the one sucked into the dark, gloomy alternate reality where paranormal is normal.

Today is a day like most days.

1

Big Hairy Deal

I'm squeezing fruit watching a crazed vendor swinging a broom in self-defense at a werewolf and I know I have to do something about it. It's my job.

With my partner we own and operate a private detective agency. We solve problems in the neighborhood. Unusual problems. No, not plumbing or electrical problems, those are someone else's problem. We deal with the who-ya-gonna-call kinda problems.

In an alternate universe I used to be an agent for the Legal Investigative Protection Service. Yes, I am the original Woman From L.I.P.S. Impressive I know, but when Matt and I were accidentally sucked into a space-time portal we ended up here where the L.I.P.s doesn't exist. A girl with my skills has to have something to do so naturally we became PI's.

Matt Butcher, former zombie, and my some time boyfriend, is my partner in our little two-person agency, Abby-Normal Investigations.

Our motto is: We take on any case no matter how weird, how supernatural, how small, how big, or how much you want to pay. Justice is our middle name.

My middle name is actually Mabel, but I hate it.

I introduce myself using only my first and last name. "Armstrong, Aloha Armstrong. Private Dick" has a nice ring to it. Aloha Mabel Armstrong? Yuk.

As far as I'm concerned my middle name is as big a secret as the combination on the suitcase with the nuclear launch codes.

Anyway, Matt and I handle the cases the cops are too scared to, or the ones they have no idea how to. Zombies, vampires, midgets (some of my best friends are midgets), swamp monsters, and all sorts of alien life forms are our traditional client base. Let me tell you aliens are the worst tippers. Anyone got change for a Zelbot drudge?

Yeah sure, every once in a while a real person walks through the door, but they're usually looking for the can.

So today, as I'm squeezing the grapefruit, this werewolf suddenly appears and starts tearing up the fruit stand and threatening to eat the customers. Since I'm a lot like Batman (other than the shoulder-length-copper-red wavy hair, knee-high-spike-heeled leather boots, leather mini-skirt, and mid-rift-barring-too-tight tee we are exactly the same), in that I carry every sort of utility item in my purse. Naturally, I come to the rescue.

I pull a werewolf biscuit from my purse and quickly have this werewolf understanding who's the alpha. In fact, soon the beast on its back whimpering like a puppy and I'm scratching its belly.

It doesn't take long before there is the inevitable shape shift and a naked woman lay at my feet and I'm scratching her belly. Ok, I know this sounds weird (and it is), but in this universe weird is my business.

I stand. "You okay?"

She blinks, with her arms and legs still in air in that aren't-I-the-cute-little-puppy position, then said, "Yeah, I think so." A frown creased her brow. "But I'm not sure."

I sense there is more to this woman's story, I just need to dig a little deeper. I need Matt.

Once back at the office I make her cup of green tea for our prospective client while Matt gives her blanket to cover herself. She's shivering by now, not a surprise given it rains most of the year. I glance out the window overlooking Bleeker street in time see a flash of lightning brighten the gray overcast sky. Really? Does it have to be gloomy all the time?

Our office is located downtown, in the seedier section of the city, in a building way past its prime. Not that it's going to be here much longer.

Foreign developers bought blocks of the seedier parts of downtown a few years back, and have built several towers worth of condos in the midst of the cesspool.

For eight hundred grand you get a closet with a great view of another closet with a great view. Did I buy one of these expensive shoeboxes? Yeah, right, I may work with the undead but I'm not brain dead.

Anyway, the woman, her name is Lizzie Harris, turns out to be an accountant for a mad scientist bent on world domination.

Why anyone would want to dominate this world is beyond me. The place is such a mess, and you'd have to spend all your time running around fixing stuff. Like I'm the handy-woman type? I don't think so.

Matt, with his calm demeanor, is, as usual, able to elicit information Lizzie doesn't realize she even knows. Square jawed Matt, with his wavy brown hair, intense hazel eyes, and aura of confident strength makes most women weak at the knees. He's beautiful and he's mine. A least for now.

In the dark days before Zombie Away, Matt suffered from zombieitis. I often wonder if his inner calm comes from his days as a zombie. He seemed so care free when we first met. Maybe if you know you're going to turn to dust soon you have a different outlook on life. I'm no shrink so what do I know?

Our on-again, off-again relationship suffers because he has no sense of humor. He's so darned serious all the time and it drives me nuts.

He says I'm too sarcastic to be a good detective. It's our sore point.

Lizzie tells us the mad scientist has been cooking the books and stealing from his investors. Who knew mad scientists had investors?

I sit half listening to her explanation of his embezzlement scheme, thinking about my hair appointment this afternoon, not particularly caring about any of this, (you invest in the evil scheme of a crazed genius what do you expect?) until she says he also applied for some government research grants under false pretenses.

"I think you just threw us a bone," I blurted silencing Matt and Lizzie.

Lizzie looked at me slack-jawed and the corners of Matt's mouth curled slightly then dropped back into the familiar grim line. He'd never admit it but I just made him laugh.

"Is that a crack?" Lizzie said indignantly.

Oops. Time for damage control. "Huh, sorry, no not at all." I tried my best let's-be-pals smile but she glared at me. Her angular features were pinched like she'd sucked on a lemon. Werewolves can be touchy about their inner wild child.

"What I'm referring to is the part about your boss ripping off the government. I don't like that."

I lowered my voice. "I mean, I really don't like that."

Lizzie shriveled deeper into the worn wing chair and gripped her tea cup tighter causing the color to drain from her knuckles. I swear I saw fear in her eyes. A frightened werewolf is just pitiful.

I may have gone too intense, but then sometimes you have to let the client know you're not all sweetness and light. It's especially important, when you're a hot looking babe like me, that people see your serious side.

Matt gazed at me and gave me the slight nod he does when he's telling me to cool it. He rolled his shoulders beneath his perfectly tailored double breasted suit, then shifted his gaze to Lizzie. "Sorry about her. She gets a little carried away." Her paused to clear his throat. "What she means is the government will pay us to find out more about your boss' embezzlement scheme."

Lizzie grinned at him like a school girl on her first date. I suppressed the urge to gag, and crossed my arms over my bosom, determined to keep quiet.

Matt continued. "What's your boss' name."

"He's quite mad you know?" Matt nodded. "His name's Tres Zero."

***

Big Hairy Deal

The Zero's had been haunting us since we started this agency. In fact even before that when we stopped the father, Arnold Zero, from stealing the formula for Zombie Away. Then we stopped his son, Uno when he threatened to turn the whole world into zombies.

A Google search confirmed Tres Zero is the illegitimate son of Uno Zero and the bearded lady from the Dingaling Brothers Circus.

Yup, we're up to our necks in zero's, again.

This simple case of embezzlement had suddenly turned into a race against time to stop another Zero from taking over the world.

My heart pounded in my ears and my blood coursed through my veins. It's s days like this when ya know this crime fighting gig just never gets old.

***

We arrived at Castle Zero, situated at the end of a windy, dirt road atop Mount Seymour overlooking the city, just as dusk fell. When you live in a place where weather is an issue let me tell you dusk falls hard. The night was as black as the inside of a cookie jar. Not that I know what the inside of cookie jar looks like, but a girl can dream, even when she's always on a diet.

Matt's driving. The '74 Pinto rattled and wheezed its way up the winding road up the side of the mountain.

Pelting rain bounced off the roof of our rusting hulk of a car. We stopped outside the ten-foot tall front gates guarding the long gravel driveway. The Pinto sighed as if were relieved to get this far.

No kidding, me too.

It often occurred to me our car might be haunted, which wouldn't be surprising, but that investigation would have to wait for another day. We had tax fraud and a take-over-the-world case going at the same time so our plate was full, thank you very much. No room for the small stuff.

Lizzie told us she'd pay mucho dollars to get the goods on her boss. And when we had the evidence of fraud we'd turn it over to the government. They pay handsome rewards for stuff like that.

I'm hoping it's enough so Matt and I can take the big vacation we always talked about—or rather, I talk about. He just listens and nods.

And then there's the whole saving the world thing. That's just icing on the cake. I mean we're talking about a mad scientist, not a rocket scientist, how serious could it be?

The Pinto's four cylinders chugged, and the fan belt whined and squeaked, as I stared through the streaky windshield at the gates.

Along the tops of the steel bars were images of hissing gargoyles and grinning fairy's with mouths full of sharp teeth. Not the most inviting thing I'd ever seen, but not the worst either.

There were those smiling clowns of Slashing, Montana. I shivered. That's an image I'd rather forget, but never could.

"There's an intercom," Matt said, with a nod of his head at the stone wall next to the gates. I squinted into the darkness. Sure enough through the shimmering rain I saw a square black pad with an oval shaped lemon-yellow button affixed to the wall about knee height from the ground.

"Oh, you've got to be kidding." This Zero is a chip of the old woodpile. The button being where it is means he's a little person. It seems in the Zero family all the fruit hangs close to the ground. "Not too far to fall, I guess," I muttered.

"What?" said Matt.

"Nothing. It's a joke."

He nodded, his face hard as steel. "You gonna get us in?"

I flipped a coin on the drive here to determine who would get out if there was a gate. I lost. I looked down at my expensive leather boots, then at the muddy road, then at Matt. I think he knew there'd be a gate.

10

I swung the car door open, then pulled my plastic rain coat over my head, and ran to the wall. Mud squished under foot and the smells of the surrounding fir and pine trees filled my senses.

Before I pressed the intercom button I noticed there was what looked like a coin slot on the panel, I hadn't noticed from the car. Odd. Never seen a coin slot on an intercom before. I shrugged and pressed the button.

I waited while rainwater dripped off my coat all around me, and shuffled my feet so my precious leather boots wouldn't sink any deeper into the sucking mud. After what seemed like forever, a gravel crunching voice came over the intercom.

"Yeah?"

I'd practiced my pitch all the way here. I knew Matt grew tired of listening when he started saying every one was pitch perfect, even though some were just stupid and off key.

"Hi, we're from Publishers Habitat Sweepstakes. We have a check for Dear Occupant." I took my finger off the button.

Girl, when your wit is on it's really on.

There was a slight pause then the voice said, "Mr. Occupant doesn't wish to be disturbed. Go away."

I pressed the button again and laughed, "No, wait. Please. That was just a little sweepstakes humor we use round the office. Actually, I have a big fat check for a Mr. Tres Zero. Would Mr. Zero be at home?" Again, I released the button.

I could feel it in my bones, this was gonna work for sure.

There was another pause, only longer this time, then the voice said, "Put fifty cents in the slot and come up to the house. Greta will meet you." The tinny speaker crackled then fell silent.

Yeah, baby you are sooo smooth.

It was then I realized I didn't have any coins on me, and for sure not in my I'm-so-cool-I'm-tiny-purse back in the car. I glanced at the slot. It didn't look like it took bills. I looked to the car with its fading headlights and sagging suspension.

I hoped Matt had exact change.

###

We came back in two hours. Thankfully, the gas station we passed at the bottom of the mountain was still open. The snag-toothed attendant even pumped gas for us so we could get the right change we needed. Ever try to pump exactly two dollars and fifty cents worth of gas? It 'aint easy.

After we got back I first buzzed the house to let them know we had returned, then slipped the coins into the slot.

I ran to the drivers side of the Pinto and climbed in as the tall gates slowly opened on squealing hinges.

Once past the gates the Pinto groaned and popped as it crunched over the gravel driveway. I winced as a rock pinged off the undercarriage. The car had to last another year, at least until I made the final payment.

Finally, we stopped on the circular driveway in front of the two-story ink-black mansion. There were stone steps leading to a heavy oak door with a gargoyle knocker. A row of twenty-foot marble columns stood on either side of the steps holding up an overhang off the sloped roof. The mansion reminded of Scarlet O'Hara's in Gone With the Wind crossed with the Addams Family house.

We got out and walked up the steps to the door. I was grateful for the overhang, it kept us out of the rain.

Matt tipped the edge of his fedora to let the excess rain fall off, (I really love when he wears his hat. It makes him look all Sam Spade.) then used the gargoyle knocker to announce us. As the echo of the thump, thump dissipated the door began to swing aside. They must have oiled the hinges recently because it did so soundlessly.

I expected the interior to be a gloomy as the exterior, but was surprised to find a well kept foyer with a polished wood floor, a maroon-navy Persian rug, and a rose wood side table with a matching chair beside it. On the table was an antique lamp that cast a soft glow over the woman who greeted us.

A gentle smile played across her thin lips. "Hello, Mr. Butcher and Miss Armstrong," she said, gazing at us over her reading glasses in a way reminiscent of a school marm. She was short—no more than four-foot eleven—with gray hair pulled into a tight bun atop her oval-shaped head. Her navy and red paisley dress, that ran past her knees, hung loosely on her small frame and on her tiny feet she wore plain black slip-on shoes.

"I'm the doctors housemaid, Greta."

"Hello, Greta," I said, deciding in the interests of time to use the direct approach I'm best known for. "We're here to see the doc. We hear he's planning on taking over the world."

A puzzled frown formed on Greta's forehead. "I'm sorry, dear but I don't know what you're talking about. Dr. Zero is trying to help people."

Matt interrupted before I could rebut the old lady. "Sorry, Greta, my partner gets a little carried away some times." He glanced at me and raised an eyebrow.

Oh, I get it. Good detective. Bad detective. I nodded but scowled at him to add to the illusion I was angry. Which I actually was, but since it enhanced my role as the bad dick I decided to play along.

Greta smiled at Matt in that creepy, cougar-like way. I swear Matt could charm the pants off Ann Coulter on her worst day.

He continued. "We've come a long way to see Mr. Zero." He patted the left breast of his suit jacket. "We have the check."

"Yes, of course. I'll take you to his laboratory." She turned and started to walk away. "Right this way."

She led us through the quiet house filled with more antique furniture, Persian rugs, the woods floors polished and gleaming. We passed a grandfather clock that chimed the half hour. The black arms on the brass face told me it was eleven-thirty already.

Finally, she led us into a massive library with floor-to-ceiling shelves filled with hard cover books. I stared at the old lady. Is she kidding? The secret entrance to a mad scientist's laboratory in the library is so old school. It's a cliché.

She walked to another door at the other end of the room then used a brass key, she withdrew from the pocket of her dress, to unlock it.

Big Hairy Deal

She swung it open and inside was the laboratory complete with a work bench with racks of test tubes, and humming machines for I-don't-know-what, and a man who could only be Dr. Tres Zero.

His lab is on the first floor, not the dusty basement? Sometimes even I can be wrong.

As I suspected, Tres Zero was a little person with slicked oil-black hair, a neatly trimmed goatee and mustache. He wore a gray vest under his white lab coat and white running shoes on his feet. To me he looked more like a miniature version of Sigmund Freud than a mad scientist, but looks can be deceiving.

"Hello," said Zero with a grin, his thumbs hooked off the pockets of his vest. A chain from a pocket watch hung across his belly between the vest pockets. "Can I have the check, please. I have a lot of work to do before midnight."

Midnight! That must be zero hour. (Com'on, you know someone had to say it.)

"What happens at midnight?" said Matt, his hazel eyes casually scanning the laboratory.

"You two and the others will be my slaves," Zero said, like he was ordering a skinny latté with a twist.

My stomach muscles tightened. We were about to take a trip on the crazy train. Good thing Matt's the boy scout of our little agency. He always comes prepared.

Glancing at the old woman I saw her being to shape shift. The old lady gave way to a snarling, flesh-eating werewolf, and I'm fresh out of werewolf biscuits.

Matt reached into his suit jacket and pulled out his .45 automatic. Without warning he turned the gun on the old lady-werewolf and shot her twice. Once in the chest, the other in the middle of her forehead. The first shot stopped her in her tracks, the other blew out the back of her head scattering her brains across the lab. The bullets slammed her backward and she landed hard then shifted back to her human form. It wasn't a pretty sight.

"Silver bullets?" I said.

Matt shrugged. "Of course."

In the commotion Zero ducked under the laboratory bench and disappeared into a trap door in the floor.

Suddenly gas jets lit up with blue and red flames along the parameter of the walls. Like all mad scientists Zero had a self-destruct-when-discovered-obsession so the house and all its contents, including the evidence of fraud, was going up in flames. If we wanted to avoid going up with it we needed to leave right now. There'd be no time to search the house.

We may have stopped Zero's evil plan for world domination, whatever it is, but our pay day was gone.

Big Hairy Deal

***

The next day we sat in the office with our feet on top of our desks discussing the Zero case, hoping the next client would soon darken our door.

"What do you think Zero was up to?"

Matt shrugged then took a sip from his Mickey Mouse coffee mug. "Werewolves I'd say."

"Werewolves?"

"Yeah, ya know a big hairy deal."

I looked at him and his features were as serious as ever. "You know you just made a joke, right?"

He shook his head. "Nope."

I sighed. "Some day you're gonna slip, and I'm gonna be there to laugh my butt off."

With Death You Get the Eggroll

I HAD JUST PARKED my rusting Lotus in front of the Ye Olde Dragon's Guild Building—my PI office is on the sixth floor of a four-story walk-up (don't ask, you don't wanta know)—when my cell phone erupted with the deep south standard, Dixie.

I immediately recognized the number on the glowing call display. Why was Owlen calling me from his cell already?

I flipped my phone open. "Where are you?"

"At the corporate headquarters of Y. O. Fortunate Message..."

I knew them. They made the little messages that went into the fortune cookies.

"We found their Vice-President of Sorcery face down in his Won-ton soup…" As usual Owlen used his best dull-investigator voice.

"Accidental drowning?"

"I dun' wanta say any more over an open phone line." The line went dead.

Owlen doesn't share my bent sense of humor. "Yeah. I'll be there in twenty," I said to myself.

I was ten minutes from resting my weary head on the pillow at the end of my ancient overstuffed couch, but now Owlen Vay had sabotaged my perfect plan. There'd be no rest for the wicked this night.

I pushed my frustration and overtired attitude deeper into my guts twisted by too much bad coffee over the last three days and nights. I knew I should have listened to the little voice inside my head whispering to stop and eat something solid. But I was too tired to eat, and too tired to argue with anyone, even my little voice.

I took a deep breath of the city into my nicotine stained lungs through the open window of the Lotus.

The warm night air of the Fraser Valley washed over me through the open car window offering to keep me awake. Most people think the smell of cauldron smog is revolting, but not me. To me it smells like ambrosia. I guess it was the big city guy bred into me by my late parents.

Maybe, rather than drive home, I should have taken up Liz's offer. Sure she was a hot dame, but I had rules concerning grateful clients. And rule number one: never sleep with a client. Sleeping with broads who pay your bills too often leads to avoidable and frequently messy complications.

It had taken me six days to cast Liz's personal demon into the hell it came from, and she was so grateful she offered me a sleep over.

I was amazed when she actually looked sad when I refused and instead accepted her healthy check. Five hundred a day plus expenses was the going rate; if I slept with every beautiful client I worked for I wouldn't feel right about taking their money. After all once in awhile even I need to eat, but man, did that doll have some gams...whew....

My oldest friend, Owlen Yonkers Vay, was my contact inside the Ye Olde Vancouver PD. He was the senior detective on the Y.O. Paranormal Investigative Service Squad—these days all companies use the Ye Olde tag at the beginning of their company name. Owlen and I shorten the tag to Y.O. because it had made the Yellow Pages obsolete. And we loved the Yellow Pages--and my former college roommate.

Long before he worked for PISS, Owlen and I attended Y. O. Magic Arts College together.

Owlen made more of himself with his degree than I ever did.

Of course, the Y. O. Mythical Creatures Equal Employment Act of 1984 had opened the doors for trolls like Owlen, and others of his ilk too often shunned by society. These days he had equal access to job opportunities like everyone else.

Owlen was one smart troll who had taken every advantage of the situation and consequently had advanced quickly within the YOVPD hierarchy.

Having a best friend who was a gumshoe, and someone capable of overlooking some of those little nuisance laws, like; 'you have no rights, scumbag' that impede criminal investigations, certainly helped him impress his superiors

Owlen and I had quite the partnership. He was the crime fighter, well I was up to my butt in dames and dough…yeah, right….I wish.

I'd only left him two hours ago and now this call. Frankly, I was worried.

This was the second card-carrying corporate sorcerer shelved in the last two weeks. Someone was peeved with the purveyors of the magical arts.

Russ Crossley

I arrived to find the glowing glass and steel twin towers of the Ye Olde Fortunate Message Corporation headquarters building protected by a phalanx of black and white police units.

After parking my car across the street from the artificial barrier of steel and flashing lights, I walked toward one of the uniforms keeping away non-existent crowds.

I didn't recognize the flatfoot outside. As you'd expect he looked bored stiff so I assumed he wasn't in the best of moods. I recognized the signs of donut deprivation in the poor guy, sleepy eyes, and a grim expression meant he must be low on sugar, fat, and caffeine.

Time to put my best foot forward. As I approached, I forced my lips into a wide smile and pulled out my identification.

Holding out my wallet, so he could clearly see my Ye Olde Licensed Investigator Association card, I said, "Rex Filagree, at the request of Detective Vay…"

The uniforms lackluster expression gave me a once over then he took the offered identification wallet from me. His gray eyes scanned the picture and my tombstone details. Without saying anything to me, he thumbed the radio mike clipped to his uniform shirt epaulette. "I gotta private dick here to see Vay…"

23

I heard Owlen's gruff voice come over the small speaker on the portable radio hanging off the uniforms black leather utility belt. "Let 'im through." The uniform grunted, stepped aside and handed me back my wallet.

I arrived at the executive penthouse to find Owlen's partner, Simone Langmack, standing leaning against the hallway wall with her arms crossed over her chest waiting for me. Her green eyes lit up and a grin crossed her tanned face when she saw me. I envied her shoulder length red curls that flowed off her wide shoulders.

Her hair always looked freshly quaffed no matter what time of day it was. She wore her usual ensemble of male-rapper-fit black slacks, two-sizes-too-large military style khaki shirt, and low heel boots, all designed to hide her figure from the casual observer.

The woman's body was one of the great mysteries of the twenty-first century. My dreams were too often filled with a longing to dig deeper into this woman's secrets.

Truth be told when Simi became Owlen's partner I'd thought about dating her, but then there was my rule number two: don't date a cop. They ask too many questions about your business.

I smiled warmly at her and tipped back my fedora with a flick of my index finger.

"Hey, Simi, you're looking fantastic as usual… where's the big guy?"

Her eyes flashed and a crooked grin crossed her high cheek-boned face. "He's inside with the vic…" she nodded at the doorway over her right shoulder.

"You kno—"

Owlen's growl cut me off. "Hey, you two, stop jawin' out there. Either get a room and be done with it, or get your butts in here and help me find this guy some justice."

Simi shrugged and whispered to me, "Even for a troll he's in a nasty mood."

I offered her a tight, but understanding, smile and nodded. I went into the room first with her following behind me.

The conference room was a large, long room.

It extended at least a hundred and fifty feet or more along the side of the office tower. There was limited lighting. The only light in the room came from a series of pot lights recessed into the ceiling that ran parallel down either side of the long conference table in the middle of the room. One wall was comprised of smoked glass. Since it was still the middle of the night, the glass reflected the glow from the pot lights blocking the view outside.

No doubt in the daytime the windows offered a terrific view of the sprawling city of parks. The building faced west and was tall enough that you could see Stanley Park and the ocean from the bank of windows on a clear day.

As I said in the center of the room was a long solid onyx table with rows of black leather office chairs on either side of the table. The set up was such that sixty executives could be seated simultaneously in the conference room, which isn't surprising given the size of a corporation the likes of Y. O. Fortunate Message. They were after all the largest manufacturer of specialty messages inserted into fortune cookies worldwide.

The messages were in reality instant spells. There were spells for love, family, money, health, happiness, luck…whatever the user needed there was an instant spell for them.

Seated at end of the long table was a figure of a man dressed in a very expensive blue pinstripe suit laying face down in a large white bowl. Slowly I walked toward what I knew to be the recently deceased Vice-President of Sorcery until I stood looking down at the unmoving body.

The pale hands rested flat on either side of the bowl.

I could very easily see the won-ton noodles floating around the head of dark hair like miniature pillows, though it was obvious this man hadn't died of natural causes. Not with the back of his skull caved in.

Once I was at the end of the table, I spotted Owlen standing next to the chair holding the body of dead executive. His wide mouth, filled with misshapen teeth, was busy mangling a stick of gum.

He quit smoking ten years ago. Since then he had the bouquet of ode de Juicy Fruit surrounding him 24/7. His red-rimmed eyes were peering into his notebook where his small, gnarled hands were busy scratching his notes.

Concentration furrowed his wide forehead. Without looking up he said, "Well, hotshot you've been here five minutes notice anything unusual?"

"Yup," I said. "No egg rolls."

***

The next morning—after five hours sleep—Owlen sat across from me behind his scarred imitation pine office desk. The overhead fan swung lazily barely moving the stifling, mould-tinged air. Cheap wooden shades covered the windows that looked out over the parking lot of the Ye Olde Paranormal Investigative Service of the VPD.

Sitting beside me was, Maury Ping, CEO of Ye Olde Fortunate Message Corporation. He was a gray haired man who looked older than his fifty-five years. He was wringing his hands as if he were continually washing them, and he fidgeted in the low-backed pleather chair. His azure eyes were angry.

"I don't get it…how could someone murder Allan? It's impossible—"

"He's dead, Mr. Ping. That's all we know with certainty," said Owlen. His gum popped. It was audible even above the squeak of the fan over our heads. "I didn't say it was murder. What I said is the death is suspicious."

Obviously, Owlen hadn't told Ping that Allan Unnoté died of headbashedinitis. Smart guy, my buddy.

Ping shook his head and removed his wire-rimmed glasses. He pinched his nose between two fingers as if he was suffering from migraine headache number forty-seven, which maybe he was.

"This is impossible…" he murmured. "What am I going to tell the shareholders…we're finished…"

I glanced at Owlen his right eyebrow was arched and his fingers were steepled across his pudgy belly. His lifted his short legs, crossed them and plopped them down on top of his desk. His shoes were unpolished. He said he was trying for the Colombo look.

Said it caused suspects to drop their guard if they thought he was a lazy slob. And I thought he was just plain lazy.

Mr. Ping was right of course. If they didn't get a new sorcerer—an interchangeable term with wizard for those who prefer—within a few days, their competitors would cast spells that would quickly cause them to bankrupt. Corporate sorcerers cast protection spells and intense defense spells to protect companies from other sorcerers.

If one company was sorcererless for even a short time it created a sorcerer-gap that other corporations would quickly take advantage of.

That's the good old free market economy for you. Rival sorcerers would create such a twisting maze of spells that by the time a new sorcerer was hired it might take weeks or months to unravel the mess. By then it was always too late.

There were rumors that some sorcerers had set up worm or virus spells that would automatically activate when a sorcerer died or left a job suddenly. Everyone knew this practice, and fear of mutual-assured-bankruptcy kept everyone in line.

The system had become so complex, and the balance of magical energy so delicate, that any disruption in the mystical continuum could have devastating consequences.

In the previous murder case, two weeks ago, the Ye Olde Wing-of-Bat-Eye-of-Newt Compotation—they made the tin take out containers for Chinese food delivery, but not the cardboard lids—went bankrupt within two days of the murder. The resulting delivery-container-gap was so serious that governments had sent in military units to make emergency delivery containers. All involved knew this was temporary and that a permanent solution had to be found and soon.

Word on the street was that several smaller suppliers were considering joining forces. As you would expect the key was whose sorcerer would be appointed Vice-President of Sorcery in the new, much larger company.

Obviously, these companies were first on our suspect list but so far we'd found no connection. If our list of suspect companies did not also produce instant spells for fortune cookies then this case worse than I first thought. It meant the culprit in both of these murders was unrelated to their competitors.

If you eliminate greed as the killers motive that leaves crimes of passion, insurance scams, or the most dreaded enemy of crime…the megalomaniac!

"Mr. Ping." I leaned forward in my chair to peer at him. "I'm sympathetic to your loss, and I appreciate what this means to your company but, sir, we have a far larger problem…"

His confused eyes locked on mine. "Like what?" he said.

"We have an unknown maniac killing sorcerers, thus it seems reasonable to suggest someone has set into motion a plan to undermine the very pillars of our civilization."

To my surprise a withering smile crossed Ping's lips. He leaned back in his chair and crossed his arms over his sunken chest. His Armani suit rustled softly in the silence.

"Yeah. Right…" he laughed. "Aren't we being a bit melodramatic, detective? I've been in this business a long time, and I've seen a lot of strange things. There was the time the Ye Olde Catch-Me-If-You-Can Corporation's wizard unleashed the Dragon of Akron. They cornered the paper plate market after that little ploy.

And then there was the Ye Olde Saucy-Sexy-Spicy Corporation, and their attempt to kidnap their competitors junior sorcerer and hold her for ransom, then—"

"There is a big difference between those friendly little competitor pranks, and murder, Mr. Ping," interrupted Owlen. "Murder is my business…"

Ping shot Owlen a look of disdain. "What would a troll know about competition?"

Such prejudicial statements weren't anything new to either of us, but this case was different. The stakes were higher and it seemed to me Ping was deliberately being confrontational. It was as if he were trying to get a rise out of us, particularly Owlen.

Owlen dropped his feet off his desk and glared at Ping. I knew he was only acting the offended party. I had seen him do this before. In reality, Owlen is the gentlest troll I have ever known.

"Mr. Ping, I suggest you keep your decorum within the limits of my tolerance while I attempt to get to the bottom of the murder of Allan Unnoté. Don't you wish me to catch the culprit?"

Ping sagged against his chair back and sighed heavily. He was like a beaten man looking into an abyss from which there is no return. "Of course, detective… I'm sorry…it's just that—"

Owlen smiled. "That's okay, Mr. Ping, you're forgiven. Now please tell us everything you know about Mr. Allan Unnoté."

***

Our interview with Ping yielded fresh fruit. We were now in the Chinese food supply district looking for the small supply company, whose name Ping gave us, where legend had it Unnoté first came to the notice of a corporate head hunter.

Ping told us Unnoté was single, forty-five, and held a Class A Wizard Certification from the Y.O. Magical Arts Bar Association.

The question raised by these facts, for Owlen and me, was how did a class A come to be socerering for such a low-level supply company? The size of this supply company was indicative of low paying sweatshops staffed by illegal immigrants. Perhaps Unnoté was an illegal?

Before we checked him out with the immigration authorities, we thought we better first check with his previous employer.

When we walked through the front door of the Ye Olde Pork Fat Palace, I thought for a second I had stepped through a time warp.

The place reeked of incense and rendered fat and there was a haze of greasy smoke.

With Death You Get The Eggroll

Unfortunately, the incense did not mask the heavy, slick feel of the place. That's about the only way I can describe the feeling of the room on the exposed skin of my hands and face.

Against one wall was a row of wooden stave barrels containing what appeared to be substances of dubious origin. The ancient walls were thick with age and stained with decades of cooking fat and the walls themselves looked to be comprised of boards peeling with age, barely able to support the sagging roof. I expected the whole kit-and-caboodle to collapse on our heads at any moment.

The owner, Mr. Benson Stein—I recognized him from the wall of employee of the month pictures behind the cash register—approached us with a wide smile in his weathered features. His gray hair was receding and would soon retreat completely. He was slim and stood no more than five foot six inches tall.

His calloused hand grasped mine as we greeted each. His grip was firm, in fact too firm. I winced behind my smile as he pumped my hand vigorously. Owlen grunted as Stein took one of his gnarled hands in his and did the same.

"How can I help you, gentlemen?"

I was relieved Stein wanted to get down to business. Skip the small talk. Good.

Owlen flipped open his badge wallet to reveal his gold shield. Stein nodded, his eyes knowing. "Yes, detective, I knew you were cops when you walked through my front door."

I wasn't surprised. Stein had been in this neighborhood for many years and probably knew everyone's coming and goings. Two strangers with paper-pusher-office hands certainly weren't locals, and we didn't dress well enough for executives or lawyers. Owlen was a little short for a health inspector. And since I was dressed in a tan raincoat and fedora, we couldn't be anything but cops, or crooks.

We hadn't stuck a gun in his face as soon when we walked in, and didn't say things like youse guys, so we weren't mobsters. This left pretty much cops. I resisted the urge to call the guy Sherlock freakin' Holmes to his face.

Owlen pulled out a picture of the late Allan Unnoté that he'd downloaded off the company's website. "We have information this man used to work for you?"

Stein took the picture and gazed at it for several seconds. "Yeah. But that was a long time ago…and…"

"What's wrong?" I noted the puzzled expression on Stein's face.

Stein frowned and flipped the picture over. The back was blank. "What's this man's name?"

35

"Unnoté, Allan Unnoté," said Owlen. "Why?"

"Well, that explains it…this isn't the man that worked for me." Stein handed the picture back to Owlen who threw me a surprised glance.

"But, sir we have information that he was recruited for the position of Vice-President of Sorcery for the Ye Olde Fortunate Message Corporation from your company—" I explained

Stein shook his head. "No. Can't be. If it is him then he looked very different, and if you know him as Unnoté then it definitely can't be the man that worked for me. His name was Kulpepper, Mark Kulpepper. And he was a sorcerer Class C. Fortunate Message would never hire a Class C for a Class A position. I mean that would be stupid." Stein shrugged. "The head hunter would have to be an idiot or…"

"What is it, Mr. Stein?" I asked. I could clearly see the wheels turning behind those black eyes.

"Well…there is another possibility…" He shook his head as if discarding the idea. "Naw. Besides it's only a rumor…"

Owlen grunted. "Rumor or not please enlighten me, Mr. Stein."

Stein considered Owlen's words. "Okay, but please don't laugh."

I crossed my heart. "I swear, and he…" indicating Owlen, "lost his sense of humor last week." Owlen winced at my lame joke.

Stein didn't seem to notice. He lowered his voice as he spoke. "There's a rumor about a mob boss recruiting Class C Wizards who are provided false documents that show they're Class A Wizards. When the corporate head hunters show up they think they've stumbled upon a real find. Reputations are made. Copious amounts of money change hands. And everyone is happy. But word on the street is in exchange for career advancement the class C's pass on corporate secrets to the mob."

Owlen looked at me and I looked at him. "No. Reaaaaally," I said.

Stein shrugged. His weathered face bore a look of disgust and he threw his hands skyward in mock surrender. "See! I knew you wouldn't believe me. After all I'm just some ignorant pork fat salesman. What do I know?"

He was about to walk away in a huff when Owlen stopped him. "Just a moment, Mr. Stein. I believe you." Owlen must have seen the surprised look on my face because I opened my mouth to speak and he cast me a look that told me I had better keep my mouth shut.

"What's this mob boss's name?"

"Huh…I was told never to say his name out loud…"

Owlen handed Stein his notebook and pen, the page was blank. "Here, write it down."

Stein took the pen and the notebook and wrote down the name. Just as he printed the last letter all hell broke loose.

###

My head was pounding like I had been on a week long bender when I woke up on the stretcher in the back of the ambulance. A dusky skinned woman with a stethoscope round her neck, and a small, sad smile on her lips, looked down on me.

"Can you understand me, Mr. Filagree?" she said.

"Huh…yeah…what happened?"

"I'm told a sneaker bomb materialized inside the former Mr. Stein's pork fat shop, and exploded…"

I raised my head too quickly and black spots danced before my eyes. I lay my head back down and groaned.

She smiled weakly. "Don't worry. You'll be fine in a few days. Good thing for you Mr. Stein was standing in front of you when the bomb exploded or you'd all be dead…"

Owlen…where was Owlen? "What about Detective Vay?"

She shook her head slowly and her dark eyes avoided me. "I'm sorry…"

My oldest friend was dead, and with him our only lead.

And I was so quick to dismiss the rumor. I wanted to curl up and die right there. But first I had to find Owlen's killer. And I knew who the chief suspect was. The mob boss, whoever he was, was going to pay….

And I knew who was going to help me get him… Simi…

As I expected, Simi was already on the scene of the burned and blackened pork fat shop working with the bomb squad and forensic technicians to sift the wreckage for evidence of the bomb making materials.

I walked purposefully up to the grim faced redhead who was so engrossed in her conversation with one of the techs that at first she didn't notice me. Sensing my presence she cut off her words and her watery eyes locked on mine.

Suddenly she wrapped her arms around me and pressed herself to me. I wrapped my arms around her. We didn't exchange any words for several seconds holding on to each as if we'd never let go. Finally, we released each other.

Stepping back, I saw the tears in her eyes. "I…" The words caught in my throat.

She placed one finger on my lips. "It's okay, Rex, we don't need to talk about this right now. We'll deal with it later."

A sense of relief washed over me. "You're right, of course, Simi."

She pulled out Owlen's notebook. It was tinged black and curled at the edges, but in the middle of the page there was written two words: The Pixie.

"Pixie? Pixie's are small winged sprites. They're friendly little creatures not mob bosses," I said.

Simi shook her head and pointed to the word 'the'. "Not a pixie, the…" she said, careful not to say the mob bosses full name. Good thing too, we didn't need another sneaker bomb going off.

"What do you know about this, pixie?"

"Plenty. Owlen has been hot on the trail of this mob boss for five years."

"He never said anything to me."

She chuckled. "You tell jokes, boyo…"

Owlen. Why did he leave me out of this investigation? Were the stakes too high? Was the risk too high? Any way you cut it, Simi and I were going to find this pixie and rip his wings off.

"Ok, where do we find this pixie?"

"A new lead came in shortly after last night's murder. I expect he was going to follow it up after you two left Steins. I think it was going to be his next sto—" Her voice cracked with emotion and tears welled up in her red- rimmed eyes. I rested one hand on her shoulder and nodded.

"It's ok," I said softly. "Let me see the lead." Simi nodded and flipped to another the charred page of Owlen's notebook.

An address. 'No. 9 Street of Dreams'.

***

We arrived on the Street of Dreams to find a faux oak door set in the heritage redbrick building that displaying a wrought iron No. 9. I was surprised it was a muffin and coffee shop called Y. O. Bubble-Bubble-Toil-And-Muffins.

Curious. I thought mob bosses usually worked from bars, strip clubs, or other similar seedy establishments. Mobsters and muffins…who would have thought?

When we went inside our senses were assaulted by the smell of fresh baked muffins and coffee. My stomach growled like a Persian pussycat in heat and I realized I hadn't eaten today and very little yesterday.

All I'd eaten these past twenty-four hours was a couple of egg rolls from a drive through place after Owlen and I left Fortunate message.

"Mind if I get something?" I said.

Simi shook her head while her green eyes scanned the shop. A large swarthy man wearing a loose fitting pale yellow golf shirt—with a Y.O. New Community Golf Course logo over the breast pocket—stood behind the counter reading a magazine. When we walked in the large man hadn't bothered to glance up to see who had entered. His bulging biceps told me this was not a man to be taken lightly.

To his right was a glass case behind which was a selection of muffins. There was acorn and apple, batwing-blueberry, sinful-strawberry, bubble-bubble-bran, and a wide variety of eclectic combinations like, dragon egg and oatmeal, and toe of lizard and lemon. That last one was too much for my low blood sugar.

My stomach twisted at the thought of the dreadful mix of flavors from some of these concoctions so I decided to go au-natural.

"Hi," I said brightly as I approached the counter. The mob guy looked over his magazine and sighed. He slapped the magazine down on the counter a withering look on his face.

"I'd like a blueberry, please."

42

He stood unmoving staring at me his dark eyes unflinching. Under his steady gaze, I felt the trickle of a single bead of sweat run down my back.

"It's ok, Sonny," said a high-pitched voice coming from floor-length gold curtain behind the mob guy whose name was apparently Sonny. "Give da guy his muffin."

Sonny grunted walked to the case and picked a blueberry off the plate of three. He snapped a plain white paper bag open and dropped the muffin into it. He wrapped his meaty fingers around the bag and squashed the muffin into a small ball then placed it on the counter.

"That'll be three bucks," said Sonny.

There was a bone-chilling cackle from behind the curtain. A six-foot tall, pixie who had to top out easily at four-hundred pounds walked through the curtain.

I studied this pixie with his royal purple curls of wispy hair on his head, and pointed ears, and thin gossamer wings sticking above his wide shoulders. The angry scar running down the right side of his face, his swollen lips, and beady eyes gave me the shivers. He was the ugliest pixie I had ever seen.

He was dressed in black slacks, and a white sleeveless undershirt. A long smoldering cigar was between his blood-red lips.

"Are you—?"

"Don't say it," said Sonny his eyes warning me.

I nodded.

"Yup, it's him," said Simi behind me.

The obese pixie's eyes narrowed giving him a truly evil appearance. "Who're youse guys?"

"Cops—" grunted Sonny.

The pixie slapped Sonny hard across the back of his meaty head and the henchman fell to the shop floor with a loud bang.

"I didn't ask you!"

"Huh…my name's Filagree. This is Detective Langmack."

A wicked smile crossed The Pixies ugly features. "I know youse…Rex Filagree…right?"

"Huh…yeah…"

"What do ya want with me?"

I felt several more lines of perspiration roll down my back. "My friend Owlen Vay was killed earlier today and we were told you might be involved…"

The Pixie grinned. His large right hand pushed the crushed muffin toward me. "Tell you what, Filagree, why don't you take the muffin on the house and get outta here before I get real angry with ya. Ok? I'd hate to see you get hurt." He winked at me.

The anger, grief, and the pure rage surfaced in me about the brutal murder of my best friend. I turned and faced Simi. She took one look at me and saw the rage in me about to explode.

Her eyes went wide as I bolted toward her and tackled her as if she were a running back carrying both of us toward the front door.

The door slammed aside with a bang. We fell to the floor and rolled toward the open door. Simi's head hit the floor hard and I saw her eyes glaze over.

"The Pixie!" I said as we went out the door. I pressed my body over hers to protect her as the bomb suddenly appeared and immediately exploded.

Shredded bits of flaming muffin shop buried us. I felt the heat of flames on my back. It took me several seconds to regain my bearings as I was still disoriented from the force of the blast.

Finally, with my lungs seemingly on fire, I rolled off Simi, slipped my burning tan raincoat off my shoulders, and kicked it away from us.

I slipped my arms underneath Simi, picked her up, and carried her away from the intense heat, smoke, and the crackling orange, red, and blue flames.

I finally collapsed to the pavement in the middle of Street of Dreams coughing and staring back at the wreckage of the Pixie's muffin shop.

I was certain no one could survive that inferno.

Simi moaned. I looked at her, slipped one hand under her head, and lifted her up. Her eyes fluttered open.

"What happened?" she said.

"The Pixie's out of business."

Her eyes went wide. "What did you do?"

A smiled weakly. "I took him out."

"Owww…my head hurts," she said.

I heard the sound of a siren. The medics would be here soon. "I know. And I'm sorry."

She smiled softly. "Its okay, Rex."

I laughed. "Ya know, Simi, I may just have broken one of my rules."

She looked at me her brow furrowed.

I laughed again. "It's ok. I'll explain later. Right now why don't we enjoy the fire."

She relaxed and looked at me with a sloppy grin on her beautiful face, her green eyes sparkling with mirth.

We sat in silenced waiting for the help that would soon arrive.

Owlen was dead. The Pixie was dead. But Simi and I were alive. And we would be responsible to carry on what Owlen started. Justice had been served.

I reached into the pocket of my pants and pulled out the baggie I had been saving. I threw it toward the dancing heat of the fire. It landed next to the flames and was quickly smoldering. Soon the plastic would melt and the contents would be consumed.

"What was that?" said Simi.

"Egg rolls."

"Why?"

I shrugged. "With death you get the egg roll."

Simi nodded. "Yeah. Egg rolls. Too bad Owlen never got his."

"Yeah. Too bad."

The Penguin Sleeps With The Fishes
A Yellow & Bird Mystery

FROM MY PERCH I watched Frank's face in the mirror over the cheaply made veneer dresser. The dresser was pushed against the wall at the end of the bed of our rent-by-the-hour hotel room. He carefully shaved the two day's worth of gray and black stubble off his product-of-the-mean-streets puss. In between strokes of the straight razor he wiped the edge of the blade on a faded gray towel, placed next to the aluminum bowl. The surface of the water in the bowel was shiny with oily soap. A smouldering Camel, stuck from the side of his cruel mouth, made me cough. The cigarette was stinking up my air.

The Penguin Sleeps With The Fishes

I shuffled down the wooden perch closer to the window and wished for the tenth time, in the past fifteen minutes, it was open. But for the tenth time it was still nailed shut. I sighed. The things I'll sacrifice for the good of our partnership. Clean air was the least of our troubles.

Good thing the window was closed actually. The summer San Francisco air outside was just above freezing. My tail feathers will freeze in ten seconds. Parrots aren't built for this kind of weather.

The only radio station in town predicted a high of forty today, but I doubted it, not with an iceberg in the harbor.

"You say sumthin', Bird?" Frank mumbled. He leaned closer to his reflection to examine his image. He squinted, swiped the blade over his face, then snorted with satisfaction. He had scraped away the last of the dark hairs with the razor.

"Naw, nunthin', Frank, just thought—"

The rotary dial phone affixed to a bracket on the of the walls covered with faded wallpaper rang. The receiver rattled in the cradle.

"Ouch!" Frank nicked his chin.

A dot of blood appeared where the scar from Oscar Ruiz's knife still showed on his chin. Old Oscar was dumb that day.

Never bring a knife to a gun fight are words I live by, and Oscar died by. Guy was good with a knife though, he had left his mark on my partner of fifteen years, before his timecard was punched for good.

I left my perch and flew to the phone. I snatched the receiver from the cradle in my left claw, then carried it back to my perch. That extra long extension cord, installed last month, really worked well. While balanced on one foot, I raised the receiver to my beak.

"FYI. Bird speaking." Even in the bad times it's good business to be polite when answering the phone. Parrots are polite.

"Bird? It's Chief. We got trouble."

I love that word. Whenever I hear the word trouble I smell a hundred a day, plus expenses.

"Yeah, Chief. What is it this week? Flaming arrows the size of Cadillac's? A flying saucer flown by a cockroach from the planet Ick who speaks five languages? Or maybe another iceberg in the harbor?"

"Enough with the jokes, Bird. This is serious. This time it's murder."

I whistled. In the mirror I saw Frank cock an eyebrow. He was busy dabbing the cut on his chin with a wad of toilet paper. I lowered the receiver from my beak and whispered, "A real case, Frank!"

The Penguin Sleeps With The Fishes

If I had opposing thumbs I would have given him a thumbs up. Instead all I could do was flap my left wing. A grin spread over his swarthy features.

"Are you talkin' to Yellow?"

"Uhhh, yeah, sorry, Chief. He's right here. Wanta talk to him?"

"Nope. All I want is you to get your feathery butt to Fisherman's Wharf, Pier 47 A-SAP. And bring Frank with ya."

Curiosity was eating me up inside. "So...who's dead?"

"Peter Penguin." The line went dead.

I stared at the receiver for several seconds, too stunned to speak.

Frank had donned his favorite powder blue dress shirt, but hadn't buttoned it yet. He was picking out a matching tie, from the three hung on a wire coat hanger in the closet, beside his two suits. My silence stopped him. He glanced over his shoulder at me. Silence is not a parrot trait, so my quiet was deafening.

He turned away from the closet and frowned. "What gives, Bird?"

I found my voice again. "The Penguin sleeps with the fishes."

***

I wasn't surprised Peter Penguin was dead.

It seemed everyone on the planet wanted him dead these days. Penguin was at the epicentre of a promotional campaign of hate, revenge, and disembowelment. During a LOX News Network Special Report, WHEN SCIENTISTS KILL, the United States Attorney General herself announced a bounty on Penguin's head. The bounty would make someone the richest person in the world. Well, the richest for a year...at least. I hope.

And in an article in Armageddon Monthly, an e-mag I subscribe to, the President, from the Oval Office at Puerto Rico White House, was quoted as saying, "Someone must kill this man."

Odd thing to say for such a nice guy as the President, but doomsday had made everyone jumpy, me included. As it turned out talk was cheap.

Now he had been murdered, and the possible suspects numbered in the billions. How were we ever going to find a killer in this haystack? It was like a broken pencil to speculate...pointless.

When the reason behind the world's poles shifting was discovered, and Dr. Penguin's Doomsday machine came to light, the doc disappeared into a rabbit hole. No one had seen him since, until today.

The Penguin Sleeps With The Fishes

Our involvement was simple. Ruby, Penguin's wife, is Franks ex. I was her pet parrot, until she tossed both is us over for the fame and fortune of being married to a Nobel prize winning egg head.

"Do you think Ruby'll be happy to see you?" Frank grunted in reply.

We stood shivering on the sidewalk in an icy wind, waiting for a taxicab.

I was perched on the padded right shoulder of his double breasted, navy blue, pinstriped suit. My wings were folded in front of my body, to provide some insulation.

The black and white Ford Whisper taxicab appeared from around the corner. The cab stopped next to the curb. The cab driver was one of those grizzled veterans of the fare wars, hunchbacked, with gray stubble that covered his leathery face, like a worn rug. He grunted, "Where to?" once Frank and I were seated in the rear compartment.

"Pier 47," I said.

The driver's beady eyes narrowed at Frank in the rear view. Frank nodded.

The driver shrugged, grunted again, then the cab pulled away from the curb smooth and noiselessly. Electric cars are quiet.

Kind of eerie in way, but who doesn't want to help protect the environment, even this close to the end of the world?

Bullet proof glass separated us from the driver, and gave us privacy. No use in setting off the celebration too soon by letting our renta-chaufer in on the good news. Ding-dong the Penguins dead, would scream from the headlines soon enough.

We didn't talk about the case anyway, just in case the driver had a mini-recorder installed to pick up some juicy gossip he could sell to the National Tattletale. Loose lips make cabbies rich.

Traffic was light. In less than fifteen minute we turned off Powell onto Jefferson, and parked at the entrance to Pier 47.

Once the car stopped Frank got out, with me still perched on his shoulder.

Frank reached in his pants pocket and pulled out his bill fold, held together by a solid silver clip, a wedding gift from his ex. He peeled off a twenty and stuck it through the small opening in the drivers window.

"Keep the change, driver." Frank smiled at me. "Courtesy of Frank Yellow Investigations." Frank handed the driver an F.Y.I business card.

The driver accepted the card and shrugged. Frank tipped the brim of his fedora and turned to walk away. I looked back as we walked away, and saw the business card flutter into the gutter, then the taxi sped away.

"Ya know, Frank, the fare was only a sawbuck. And I've been eating a lot of budgie seed lately."

Frank nodded. "Yeah, I know. The cabbie may need our services some day. Think of it as a promotional expense."

I pictured the image of our business card landing in the icy gutter. "Yeah. OK." Frank never could read people very well, but then the detecting part of our partnership was my job.

As we approached the arch over the entrance to Pier 47 we were greeted by two penguins. There was the irony of penguins living in San Francisco, where Peter Penguin's body turned up, but they were illegal aliens, and Peter Penguin was a citizen.

Penguin is not one of my languages so we steered well clear as we walked under the arch and onto the deserted pier. Good thing too, because the smell of dead fish was thick even at this distance. Personally, I've never understood eating anything except seed, but what do I know? Parrots aren't gourmet cooks.

The Chief appeared down the pier. He wagged his tail when he spotted us. "Over here, Bird...Yellow!"

The coroner, Lars Pederson, appeared from a doorway.

His normally pale cheeks were rosy from the cold, and the hood of his parka was pulled over his short blond hair. Frank quickened his pace and we hurried past darkened t-shirt, jewellery, and souvenir stores. The shop owners had left San Francisco long ago. What creeped me out was the shops were still stocked, as if the people had suddenly disappeared. The world had become one of those B grade science fiction movies. Only this wasn't a movie, this was real.

I stayed in San Francisco because it's my home, and Frank needs me. Besides where am I going to go?

Lars took Frank's hand in his, he shook it vigorously. If you didn't know them you would have thought they were just trying to keep warm, but the two men had been friends back to their days at PS 32, in Brooklyn. They launched into one of those let's-catch-up conversations.

"Polly want a cracker?" I looked down to see Chief next to Lars. Chief was a five-year old Jack Russell terrier. He's a small dog with a big chip on his shoulder. Trouble with a capital T. I rolled my eyes. "Very funny, Chief."

Chief laughed gruffly. Some things never change. "Where's the body?"

Chief nosed Lars' left leg. "Lars, show Yellow and Bird our victim."

I didn't like the tongue in cheek quality to his tone. After all a man had been murdered, and the killer was still on the loose.

What kind of leg humper are you, Chief?

Lars nodded, then he led us into the store he'd just come from. It was a movie memorabilia store. The walls were covered with movies posters, and there were racks of DVD's. Glass stands, that contained rows of action figures and celebrity bobble heads, lined both walls. Everything was covered with a layer of dust, and the floor was covered in sand. Without the sand the wood planks would have been a skating rink.

Only this ice smelled like wet corpse.

Lars led the way to the back of the store. Behind a counter, where I presume the cashier used to stand, though the cash register had been removed, leaving behind ragged holes where the register had once been, was the body of the late Professor Penguin.

He lay spread eagled on his back, his face the color of chalk, his bloodless lips blue. He was dressed in a tuxedo. Hmmm...a penguin in a penguin suit. Irony had reached new heights.

In the center of his chest, about where his heart was, was a dark round hole, obviously the entry point of the bullet that killed him. Good shootin', tex...

Frank dropped to his haunches, and flicked his fedora back on his forehead with his index finger. I flew to the counter to land near the edge. I wanted a bird's eye view of the crime scene.

"How long has he been dead?" I asked.

"Don't know, Bird," answered Lars.

I turned my head so one eye faced the lanky coroner. "Why not?"

He shrugged. "He's been in the water too long."

"Water? What are you talkin' about, Lars? He's in here, not in the bay." I glanced at Frank. He regarded me with an annoyed look in his eyes. Frank was right. Something's fishy, and its not the penguins by the entrance to the pier.

"Ok...Chief what's this all about?" Frank stood and glared at the terrier. The cops in this town had gone to the dogs.

"We were hopin' you guys would know." Chief's gruff voice was even, and his eyes were serious.

Thanks, Chief, you just threw me a bone. "He means he thinks we plugged the Penguin, Frank."

Frank smirked. "Com'on, Chief. We're law abiding citizens. You know that."

Chief's eyes sagged and he sat back onto his haunches. "You're right, of course. But I'm baffled. The clothing and the body are soaked in salt water, but we found him in here. We're stumped."

"Who called it in?" I asked.

"A woman. She didn't leave her name. We traced the call to a phone booth on Clay Street. Nothing."

My brow wrinkled. "Was there any identification on the body?"

Chief looked at me with that are-you-pulling-my-hind-leg expression. Yeah, everyone on the planet knows Peter Penguin on site.

"No." It was Lars who spoke this time. "But we did find this..."

He handed me a plasticized business card. It read, MADAME YBUR, PALM READER, MEDIUM. Odd name. Must be Iraqi. "Mind if I keep this?"

The address on the card was on Kearney, not far from Clay. The madam's name twigged something in my memory.

Chief nodded. "Sure. We already checked it out. The old lady is goofy, but not goofy enough to kill anyone."

"Thanks." I gave the card to Frank who pocketed it. Parrots don't have pockets.

We said our goodbyes and started to walk back to the street. Along the way Frank lit a cigarette. I rolled my eyes as the acrid smoke wafted over me. "When are going to give those up? They'll kill you."

Frank snorted. "What difference does it make now?"

He had a point. "But if that were true, Frank then we may as well lay down right now and die. Remember, we're trying to solve a murder because we want to, not because we have to. There's a big difference."

I shifted tactics. "Frank, what if you were with Ruby again? She hated when you smoked."

Frank shrugged as he took a long drag from the Camel before answering. "Yeah, you're right. I guess I'd quit." He chuckled. "But that's not going to happen, Bird. You can bet your yellow and green butt on that."

"I'm not so sure about that."

###

We arrived in the same taxi as the one that had dropped us off at Pier 47. The driver was the same. And he had the same dislike for customers. Frank acted like they were old friends.

We arrived at the address in a few minutes. When we got out the driver seemed to drive away faster than the first time. Fifteen dollar tips don't buy what they used to.

It didn't help that Frank had to pay him with a combination of dollar bills and quarters, and the tip was only twenty-five cents.

I rolled my eyes at Frank. He blushed. Big man, throwing around fat cash as if we had any. "Let's find Madame Ybur. I need a drink so I want to get to the nearest watering hole as soon as possible."

Frank and I entered through the revolving glass doors to the lobby. The lobby was a combination of smoked glass, gleaming chrome, and marble, In the middle of the lobby was a wide pond. A tall palm tree, heavy with coconuts, sprouted from amongst a jungle of smaller plants on an artificial island in the center of the pond. Beautiful.

In one corner of the lobby was a kiosk, like the ones at the mall. Only this kiosk didn't sell knock off watches, or Japanese animé action figures. This kiosk was for matters related to the occult, palm reading, and a medium who would contact your loved ones on the other side. Given recent developments a medium might be a useful skill, if it wasn't a scam.

Next to the kiosk, sitting on a wooden stool, was a dark haired woman dressed as a gypsy. Business was slow so she had her eyes buried in a novel. It must have been a good book because she didn't look up until were stood over her.

From my perch on Frank's shoulder I could see the book was a romance.

She looked up into Frank's eyes and the initial surprise was quickly replaced by joy. Her look was enough to warm the cuckolds of my heart. If I was human. But I'm a parrot, we have different tastes.

"Madame Ybur?" I asked from my perch.

Madame Ybur laughed. What did I say that was so funny? "Sorry. It's just funny to hear you say my name backwards."

Backwards? Ruby! Ruby...Peter's wife...Frank's ex-wife...Peter Penguin's dead...Frank...Ruby...oh, oh...

Before I could stop them, I was forced to fly off Frank's shoulder as Ruby and Frank rushed at each other. They locked in a passionate embrace. They're lips were glued to each others and their arms were wrapped around each other bodies. No doubt the only thing that would separate them now was a fire hose on full blast.

Since I wasn't about to do that that I flew to the kiosk and landed. I folded my wings and waited.

Looking around the kiosk I saw the typical trappings of the paranormal huckster.

Books on metaphysics, crystals in various shapes, baby food-sized jars that contained a rainbow of colored powders. It was a real fraud-fest.

The Penguin Sleeps With The Fishes

And with the bunko squad on permanent vacation Ruby was going to be successful with her fraud. Not that it mattered. Doomsday was just around the corner.

Then, of course there was the murder of Peter Penguin. I spotted the butt of a gun sticking from under a sheet of paper on the kiosk's counter top. And next to the gun was a voodoo doll with pins sticking from the center of it's chest.

As I suspected Ruby, who spelled her name backwards for the purpose marketing her disguise as a tarot card reader, murdered her husband.

My problem now was do I ruin what's left of Frank's life and turn her in, or do I ignore his happiness and call Chief?

I made up my mind immediately. At least Frank will stop smoking.

The things I'll sacrifice for the good of our partnership, and our friendship.

It was the end of the world as we know it, but love would endure forever. And I'll be breathing clean air. Besides I'm a parrot not a stool pigeon.

Sorry, Chief.

Five Minutes

Bump looked up from the newspaper he'd been studying into the green-gray eyes of the red haired waitress standing staring expectantly at him. Her dye job did nothing to disguise she was older than she wanted to be. The oval patch over the sagging left breast of her white uniform blouse read *Thelma*. He assumed this was her designation.

Bump considered it sad that in his line of work the only women he met had to work past their expiry date and were usually damaged goods. His was a rotten business and sometimes he really hated it. But this particular job meant he had to locate another type of woman. A woman with a deadly agenda.

Only he hoped the woman he'd been paid to find wasn't as world weary as this one. If she was then she wouldn't care about her life or anyone else's. These type of targets were the scariest kind. He really hated those jobs, but a guy had to make a living didn't he?

"What'll it be?" she said her voice rough from too many smoke breaks.

Sometimes he'd forget how many people smoked in the twentieth century. In his day no one smoked. Smoking had been banned long ago.

Too bad he hadn't time before he left to have dummy tobacco sticks made up. He'd have to say he didn't smoke which would put his cover in jeopardy each time he said it. His recollection from his college history class about the middle of the twentieth was everyone smoked. Children as young as five or six started smoking, then they were hooked until they died of smokers cough. At least that was how he remembered it. But he could be mistaken, he wasn't much of a student

Regardless, his plan was he'd be out of here before he had to tell anyone he didn't smoke.

"How 'bout your phone number?" He hoped she didn't say yes because he'd never used a telephone and he had no idea right now how long he'd be in this time.

Her gray eyes narrowed and her mouth formed a sneer. "'Aint on the menu, buster." She stuffed her pad and pencil into the pocket in the front of her apron tied around her waist. She turned around and retrieved a white coffee cup from a stack on a counter under the stainless steel pass bar that separated the cook from the waitress.

On the other side of the open pass bar was the white haired cook in a white cotton undershirt. He sported two missing teeth and hadn't shaved in a couple of days evidenced by the uneven gray stubble on his street weary face. An angry scar ran across his chin and up the left side of his face.

Thelma cocked an eyebrow at him. "Coffee?"

Bump smiled. "Yeah. Sure. Thanks."

She snorted as she turned her back to him. "Don't be thanking me until you've tasted this mud."

"You watch yor mouth, T," said the cook gruffly from the kitchen.

The coffee shop was empty at this time of day. Evidently no one fancied greasy spoon food at three in the morning.

Thelma smirked and selected a white porcelain cup from a stack next to the large steel coffee percolator on the counter then held the cup under a spigot and filled the cup with black coffee.

Five Minutes

She set the full cup in front of him. His nose wrinkled at the smell of over cooked beans cut with too much chicory.

He recognized the smell from his days in the marines when he was stationed in the outer worlds. They used to cheap out the military in those days. The days before the second great war. A buddy who'd stayed in sent him an e-note once telling him how jarheads ate steak every night and drank gourmet coffee.

Bump never heard from the guy again so he assumed he'd become fodder in the seemingly endless war to end all wars. At least he left on a full stomach topped off with some decent coffee. Not like this foul swill was sure to taste.

He folded the newspaper in half and lay it on the coffee counter and searched the counter for the sugar and salt and pepper shakers. There were none in evidence. "Sugar?"

"You're kiddin' right?"

He remembered now. Milk, sugar, flour and salt were rationed but he didn't remember why. And he couldn't recall at the moment who the enemy in this war had been. He glanced at the headline on the folded newspaper. Duhhh. Nazi's. Of course.

"Do you have any milk?" he said politely as possible

A sardonic smile played across her lips and she went to a large refrigerator standing at the end of the counter shoved against a wall next to the swinging door to the back. She came back with a glass bottle half filled with milk.

She tipped it and whitened his coffee. He smiled at her. "Thanks."

'Where you from, mister?" Thelma said when she came back from putting the milk bottle away.

Oh, oh. Now what? "Why would you think I'm not from around here?" he said keeping his voice as even as possible.

She eyed him suspiciously. "You talk funny and your clothes are wrong."

Bump sat back against the back of the chair and chuckled. "Well, well how 'bout that. Nothing gets past you does it, Thelma?"

She scowled at him and looked about to leap across the counter at him. He'd insulted her. He'd never been skilled at sarcasm. Not good. She'd soon begin to think he was a Nazi too.

"Sorry. What I meant was you're right. I'm visiting. I'm from Chicago." It was a lie but certainly preferable to the truth.

Thelma's features softened. "American, eh? What ya doin' here?"

"I'm a private investigator. I'm trying to locate someone. Name's Bump McShott."

Thelma turned her head toward the kitchen and yelled, "Hey, Archie, Sam Spade is in the shop."

"Tell him he's gotta order sumthin' like everybody else," called Archie from the kitchen.

Thelma offered him a thin smile. "Archie don't go to the movies much."

Bump wondered what a movie was and who how he'd been mistaken for a guy named Sam Spade. He thought about correcting her but her eyes had the spark that meant he'd found his way in to her camp. Problem was he had no idea what a movie was.

He made a mental note in future he should do better research before coming this far back. Unfortunately, this job's timeline didn't allow sufficient time to do the necessary research. All he'd been able to do was find a vessel to inhabit for the twenty four hours he needed to track Pinky Ames and to stop her.

The time table said he'd only have five minutes after he found her but his one strong asset was over confidence born of success. It was why he accepted the hefty pay day, if he achieved the objective. His business was result-based so it was feast or famine. And famine usually meant paradoxes for someone.

So far he hadn't created any personal paradoxes, at least none he was aware of.

He smiled at Thelma and took a sip from the warm coffee mug. He winced when the acidic brew burned his tongue. He was thankful when his taste buds were burned because it meant he couldn't taste the stuff. He'd drunk coffee during other assignments and the stuff was an acquired taste he'd never acquired.

Thelma leaned her elbows on the counter and stared at him with a thin smile on her lips. "You're not from Chicago are you, Bump?"

He believed the popular jargon of the period in this circumstances' went; 'The jig is up.' He had no idea what a jig was but somehow it fit this situation. "No. Not Chicago," he said slowly, keeping his eyes fixed on hers.

Thelma straightened up after removing her elbows from the counter then crossed her arms over her bosom. "I know who you are because I'm also not from Chicago." She nodded toward Archie who was visible over the stainless steel pass bar in the kitchen. "And neither is Archie."

"What year?" Bump asked. It was along shot but something about the way they talked told him they were out of period too.

A shadow of a smile played across her lips and her eyes narrowed. "2434. You?"

"2418," Bump replied. "Kinda crowded in the past these days don't ya think?"

Thelma smirked. "Yeah. Sure is." Her brow wrinkled. "Corporate, government, or private?"

Bump set the mug on the counter then reached over ad pulled a paper napkin from the dispenser. He wiped his mouth with the napkin then crumpled it in his fist. "Private. Like I said I'm a private investigator."

Thelma's thick, dark eyebrows formed twin arches on her forehead. "Really? You really a PI?" He nodded. She chuckled and shook her head. "Me and Miles are on holiday. You sure look the part in that rain coat and the fedora."

Bump grinned. These two were rich morons on a lark.

Somewhere in their program was an automatic retrieval worm if they tried to change history. Any attempt to assassinate Hitler, or provide future technology to someone in the past resulted in automatic retrieval, a hefty fine and prosecution. There had been a few cases where the death penalty had been handed out but most often the offender was subjected to a memory wipe.

Since the entire purpose of vacation time travel was to see and interact with the past, and share the experiences at parties, a memory wipe was considered a sufficient deterrent.

The idle rich were the customers of the time travel corporations so they stayed in line with the rules.

Bump had lost count of the number of times he wished for a memory wipe, but while his trips were privately funded they were hardly vacations so he was allowed some leniency in the application of the rules. And the Time Enforcement Agency had thus far been unable to tie him into any disruption to the timeline. The corporations who hired him had friends in high places to take care of his missteps.

Bump reached into the pocket inside his suit jacket and pulled out a black and white photograph. He showed the smiling woman depicted in the photograph to Thelma.

"You seen her in here? Or has anyone mentioned an Arlene Bennett to either of you."

This diner was near the debarkation wharf where the troop and cargo vessels docked to refuel and load with men and material for war. Just about every sailor that had ever come through the port had come into this diner.

Five Minutes

Bump assumed this was why Thelma (obviously not her real name) and Miles (disguised as Archie) wanted to be here. They'd get a wealth of experiences from the sailors who came through to brag about at parties.

Surprisingly Thelma scoffed. "Archie, get out here."

She must have become accustomed to using her companions cover name because she sneered it in the sincere way people who believed what they were saying. These two had clearly done their research before coming back.

Bump stuffed the picture of Arlene Bennett back inside his suit jacket just as Archie came through the swinging door. A grease stained white apron covered his clothes and trails of dirty sweat streaked his puffy freckled cheeks. Sitting atop a nest of tight oil-black curls he wore a round white hat. His jaw was tight with undisguised anger.

Bump swallowed hard. This man was a tough customer.

Thelma looked at him with a sneer ion her face. "Throw this guy out, Arch."

"What? Why?" said Bump. He remained seated as Archie rounded the end of the counter and came at him.

He realized he wasn't getting an explanation when Archie spun the stool around and grabbed by him shirt collar and his belt and yanked him to his feet. Spots danced before his eyes due to the sudden application of force to his windpipe.

Bump estimated Archie had a good fifteen kilos on him so he knew struggling would be pointless, and would likely result in a black eye or a broken bone or two. Any serious injuries would delay his mission and he'd miss his window of opportunity. Missing an assignment was unacceptable to his employer and would result in disciplinary action.

He smiled to himself. Too bad discipline meant a single shot to the head. Not that he was worried, his success rate of one hundred percent and holding was in the corporations and his best interest to maintain. The corporations didn't wish to attract unwanted attention from the certain government agencies if his assignments went awry. Of course he'd be the one to suffer the most but any corporation with a prohibition to mine the past would soon enter bankruptcy. The arrangement was symbiotic but deadly in its implications.

Archie raised so his feet no longer touched the floor and carried him toward the front door of the diner.

Five Minutes

Bump gagged and sputtered waving his arms as the heavily muscled time traveler-slash-cook carried him to the door. Once at the door he was dangled in mid air for what seemed to be an eternity. His vision blurred as a lack of oxygen starved his brain. He heard Thelma heels click on the dirty tile floor until she came into view and swung the door open. She offered a tight lipped smile and waved her fingers at him just before Archie tossed him out the door where he landed hard on his butt on the rain soaked sidewalk.

He gasped for air and spots danced in front of his eyes as he managed to drag the first few breaths into his tortured lungs. Slowly his breathing normalized. His butt was wet and it hurt like hell.

His day wasn't going as he'd planned that much was clear. But unanticipated violence was in the job description.

After managing to stand on shaky legs he stumbled into the alley across the street from the diner. Daybreak was still several hours away so he had little concern he'd run into trouble in the alley.

With his mind now clear, Bump decided to stay where he was to observe who arrived in the diner after his abrupt departure. The alley was shrouded in shadow so he wouldn't be seen by anyone walking by.

In contrast the diner was well lit from inside. He would have a perfect view of anyone coming and going in the diner. Her saw Thelma and Archie moving about their movements frantic and nervous. They reminded him of birds in a cage. It seemed they had lost their courage after their rough treatment of him.

Right now they were looking mostly to the west toward a row of three story brick apartments farther down the street. Evidently, something about Arlene Bennett had unnerved them.

He didn't have to wait long because a woman wearing a scarf over her dirty blonde hair appeared huddled in a long wool overcoat rushing toward the diner. She entered through the diner's door. The echo of tinny bell over the door drifted on the cold winter air to him standing in the alley. He shivered.

The woman was immediately met by Thelma and Archie who appeared highly agitated given how they spoke rapidly and waved their hands about to as if to emphasize what they were saying. Now he understood his treatment. These two were conspirators with Arlene Bennett and this woman had to be Arlene, the subject of his investigation.

Five Minutes

Bump considered bursting into the diner and apprehending her but this would not stop whatever plan her employer had in mind, he or she would just send someone else. And he'd not discover the identity of the person who hired her. His information was she had been hired by a corporation, she wasn't an agent of an official body.

Now raised, angry voices drifted through the windows of the diner. Bump smiled to himself. His appearance had upset their plans. "Good," he mused under his breath.

Finally Arlene left the diner, after slamming the door hard behind she walked briskly headed toward the row brick apartment buildings that abutted the dock area.

Bump stepped out of the alley and began to follow her keeping a discrete distance between them. He ducked into another alley when Arlene stopped to look for anyone following her. He held his breath and stole a quick look around the wall and to see she once again had started walking. He started after her keeping his distance and using any shadows he encountered to cover his tailing her.

They had walked nearly an hour and were in an area of the city unfamiliar to him.

The buildings were still made of brick, mortar and stone but they were higher and more ornately decorated along the roof line with scrolls and carved stone statues of gargoyles and other mythic creatures.

Finally they arrived at the apparent destination because Arlene entered one of the buildings using a key she pulled from her coat pocket.

She closed the door behind her and he heard the echo of the lock being turned.

Bump waited several seconds then rushed to the door. As he suspected it was locked.

He grunted softly in frustration then scanned the street to see if anyone was watching him. Delivery trucks had started moving on the streets but there were no pedestrians on the sidewalks at this still early hour.

Looking back to peer at the lock in the door handle, Bump reached into the pocket of his overcoat and pulled out a small red disc-shaped object. He placed the disc over the keyhole in the door and there was a soft click. Taking one last look both right and left at the street and seeing no one he swung the door inward and, after pocketing the disc, slipped inside closing and locking the door behind him. He had to be careful not to let anyone of this period see the lock pick.

Five Minutes

Since he had no idea where in the twenty story building Arlene would be he decided to check the directory to see if he recognized any names from the thin briefing file he'd been provided. Naturally he'd used his usual back door sources to augment what he was provided, and to determine exactly who he was working for. He needed to know of the true objective of his mission.

Bump hadn't survived fifteen years in this business without discovering the hidden agenda of his employer. He was fairly sure every corporation that hired him knew he did this but they never said anything since he got results.

In the low light coming form the beginnings of dawn coming through the lobby windows he Bump scanned the names listed alphabetically on a brass plate set in the wall between the two elevators.

His heart froze and he took in a breath when he came to a name he recognized. Robert Shaw, MD, Room 1012.

Dr. Shaw was the ancestor of his employer, Hart Shaw CEO of Light Drive Technologies. Arlene was here to kill Dr. Shaw. But why?

***

When he arrived at the office door of Dr. Shaw, Bump saw there was light coming from under the door.

The rest of the building was deserted so this had to be where Arlene had come.

Resting his ear against the door he managed to make out muffled voices. Good. Arlene hadn't left so Dr. Shaw must still be alive.

Bump slowly tried turning the doorknob, but like the lobby door it too was locked. He cursed under his breath. The elevator motors broke the silence startling him. His heart beat rapidly and his mouth dried.

He was running out of time the early starters had begun to arrive. Bump ran his tongue across his lower lips then took out the lock disc and placed it on the Dr. Shaw's door lock.

It was risky to burst into the room. If Arlene had a weapon trained on Dr. Shaw she'd kill him before he could stop her. And then his employer would be gone and then a paradox for him and death for a whole line of Shaw's and who knew how many others. He would need toy proceed with caution, even if it meant his own death.

Bump heard the lock disengage then he slowly swung to door in. The light inside went out.

"Hello?" he said as the door opened. "Dr. Shaw?"

"Come in and close the door behind you," said a husky woman's voice. It must be Arlene.

Five Minutes

As Bump's eyesight adjusted to the low light coming through drawn shades over the windows the shrouded image of a someone standing next to a chair with another person seated became distinguishable.

"Dr. Shaw?" he said again.

"Dr. Shaw is tied up at the moment. What do you want?"

"Uhhh, I need some medical advice."

Arlene chuckled mockingly. "Yeah. Nice try. Dr. Shaw isn't a medical doctor so you may as well leave."

Bump smiled to himself. "Sorry, you and I both know I can't do that." Bump moved to the right side of the door and found a light switch on the wall. He flicked the switch and the overhead light in the middle of the ceiling. He blinked and recognized Dr. Shaw seated on a wooden chair. His arms were tied to the chair with black electrical cord and a cloth had been stuffed in his mouth. Bump recognized him because his future great, great, great grandson looked exactly like him.

He hadn't been harmed but that was about to change. On the floor underneath the chair was a bomb, a bomb he recognized. When it went off it would implode everything within five feet. Since it was designed to implode upward Dr. Shaw and the would disappear forever.

Russ Crossley

It would be like he never existed which seemed poetic.

"How long?" he said simply gazing into Arlene's eyes.

Her eyes were dark as a pool of water at night and her expression was placid, unconcerned. Her attitude unnerved him. But he was determined not to show she'd gotten to him.

"It has a five minute timer. We have four minutes and thirty eight seconds to get out."

He knew exactly what she meant. They'd leave these bodies, that would be consumed by the blast, and their own consciousness would return to their own time. It concerned him that he and Arlene might not exist in the future since the timeline would have been altered, but that was the risk of corporate espionage in the past.

Sometimes he wondered what reality was anymore. With all the time travel going on reality had probably changed so many times that truth had little meaning.

He and Arlene could have played out this cat and mouse game many times, and every time the result would have been different.

"What corporation you working for?" he asked to keep the conversation going.

83

Five Minutes

By his mental calculation they had four minutes and thirteen seconds.

Her mouth formed a half smile. "Not working for them."

He nodded at the terrified Shaw who struggled to free his arms. The chair rocked side to side. With sufficient time he'd probably have gotten free but there wasn't time. "Then why?"

Her eyes became hard and her mouth became a grim line. "Personal reasons."

Bump arched an eyebrow. "Really? Tell me."

"Why should I?"

"Well, for one reason in three minutes and forty one seconds we're all going to die or you and I will disappear in a paradox. So I say why not?"

Surprisingly, she smiled. "Sure. Why not?"

A bead of sweat trickled down Bumps shirt collar.

Three minutes and fifteen seconds.

"Dr. Shaw will have three sons. Two become doctors, psychiatrists like himself, while the third becomes a train engineer. These three men marry and each have two children. Of these the records are somewhat murky due to a paradox but our record does show one boy grows up to found a black market munitions company."

"So his ancestor killed your family, right?" interrupted Bump.

She scowled at him. "Don't be ridiculous. Do you want to hear the story or not?"

Two minutes and thirty one seconds.

"Yeah, sure. Sorry."

"So, as I was saying my father—"

"Your father?" He couldn't help himself.

"Yes," she crossed her arms over her chest. "My father's company was founded as a munitions company selling arms to the highest bidder. The money made is tainted with innocent blood."

"So you want to clear your conscience is that it?"

"No, it's too late for that."

"But your father's company now manufacturers faster than light drives and has helped humanity to travel the stars and open up trade with countless worlds across the galaxy. That's not so bad is it?"

One minute and twenty five seconds.

"Unless you've seen the future then I would say you're correct."

Bumps heart froze. Travel to the future was illegal and highly dangerous. Tampering with future events could have disastrous consequences for the past.

She smiled.

One minute and one second.

"What has Dr. Shaw got to do with this?"

"As I said he will have three sons."

So that was it. Wipe Dr. Shaw from existence, no children, and no Shaw's, including Arlene, or whatever her name was.

Forty one seconds.

"You know you'll be gone too, right?" She nodded. Then he realized she wasn't leaving before the implosion.

Thirty eight seconds.

He fought the urge to ask her what she'd seen in the future but he knew in his gut he didn't want to know. No one should know. What he did know was Arlene was willing to sacrifice herself to save the future.

Twenty nine seconds.

He paced the room. "I have to know, Arlene."

"My name's Ariel Shaw actually," she said.

Twenty five seconds.

"Well then, Ariel I have to be sure I'm doing the right thing."

"I know I'm right. I saw it with my own eyes," she said.

Bump gazed into her eyes. Does he trust her? He had to do what was right.

Eighteen seconds.

Bump looked at Dr. Shaw and saw the raw fear in his eyes. He blinked away the sweat trickling into his eyes. Did he deserve to die to save the future? Did anyone?

Eleven seconds.

"How about I take Dr. Shaw back with me?" Bump suggested.

"Is that even possible?"

He shook his head. "No."

Eight seconds.

"Are you going to stop me?" Ariel asked.

"No." In truth he hadn't fully decided.

Three seconds.

With one second to go Bump decided. He triggered the return worm in the program and woke up in the travel chamber.

He breathed a sigh of relief. He was still here. No paradox. As he stepped out of the chamber and headed for the showers since he'd been in the chamber for the past twenty four hours.

The memory of the last twenty four hours began to fade as he stood under the spray of the hot shower. By the time he finished it was gone.

Five Minutes

All it took was five minutes and the past was gone forever.

Bump looked forward to his next assignment and wondered where and when it would take him.

One Red Shoe

O PERATIVE MADDIE SUREFOOT studied the shoe. It was sure a big one, at least twenty feet high. She'd never seen one like it before. It looked familiar but she didn't know where she'd seen it before. All she knew for sure was she had seen this shoe before.

Reaching inside her cotton suit jacket she pulled out her cell phone from her inside pocket and pressed the quick dial number for her section chief.

Barb Wallup's voice answered after one buzz at the other end.

"Maddie. What's up?" She sounded impatient. The boss must be having a bad day.

Maddie had already considered the summary of what she'd seen in her mind before she made the call.

"Hi, Barb, I'm at the scene now and it's exactly as reported by eyewitnesses."

Barb snorted. "I thought I'd seen everything." The chief paused. Maddie knew what was coming. "Any idea how it got there?"

The million dollar question. She had considered all possibilities, but nothing she'd thought of made sense expect one, and she didn't want to think about that. "No. There doesn't appear to be any reasonable explanation. So far."

"How about unreasonable explanations?"

"If you mean do I have a theory then, yes I might have one."

There was silence on the other end of the line. A pauses that spoke volumes. Barb Wallup was a practical woman who liked her explanations clean and simple. The Internal Secrets Bureau collected and hid many strange things from the general public, but everything had a rational explanation as far as Barb was concerned, no matter how fantastic.

"Ok, Maddie, try me."

Maddie sucked in a breath then let it out slowly. "I think this is the home of the woman who lived in a shoe, who had so many children she didn't know what to do."

There was a long pause. So long in fact, Maddie began to think Barb had hung up. Finally her chief asked, "You know what this means don't you?"

Maddie swallowed hard as her heart rate increased finally she said, "Yes. It means the giant is back in town."

Rednose the giant hadn't been seen in fifty years. If this was his shoe it meant he and his wife Brunhilda had been fighting again and the shoe had been tossed out of his kingdom on the other side of reality.

The land of unreality was the realm where there were giants, elf's, unicorns, and goblins, wizards and witches, and other creatures too terrible to dream of. The barrier between reality and unreality hadn't been breached since the beanstalk was cut down five decades ago.

Before she married her father, Maddie's mother, Irish McComb, had been an ISB operative. Irish had chopped down the beanstalk in time to stop the invasion of reality by unreality.

These days it would be simple if all the ISB had to deal with were vampires, alien invaders, or giant mutant insects, but an invasion from unreality? That was every ISB operatives worst nightmare.

One Red Shoe

Maddie's mother had saved reality barely in the nick of time, this time her daughter might not be so lucky. Too bad the cameras in those days were the size of a terrier and her mother had dropped hers while trying to climb down the beanstalk so fast or they'd have pictures of the giant and his castle. A lay of the land would be very useful of they were going to plan an adequate defense.

If the chief had her way they'd be planning a full scale preemptive assault rather than defense, but Maddie convinced Barb there was a better way than war.

Maddie stood on the cement walkway looking up to the porch that ran along the Victorian style house that was known to the world as the Shade Tree Seniors Residence. (STSR is the cover name for the Retired Spies, Saboteurs, and Terrorists Rest Home and Bingo Emporium. Apparently retired spies, saboteurs, and terrorists love to play bingo. Who knew?)

Maddie clipped the alligator clip attached to the top edge of her ISB identification badge to the breast pocket of her suit jacket. She took a deep breath then released it. She hadn't visited her mother for two months, so she'd have to listen to complaints about what a bad daughter she was.

Russ Crossley

She could hear her mother saying that just because Maddie was off on dangerous secret missions, facing death at every turn, didn't mean she couldn't find time to visit her elderly mother.

Since every internal organ in her mothers body had been replaced, and she'd been genetically enhanced in every way known to medical science, Maddie's mother was far from elderly. But nevertheless Maddie'd hear about her less than exemplary offspring skills.

She arrived at the front door of what looked to passersby as just another ordinary house on an ordinary street in an ordinary small town in America. What the world didn't know was behind this door was the most modern facility yet built to house the retired veterans of the secret wars of the past eighty years.

The door had no doorknob and there was no mailbox. The windows old fashioned wood framed windows on either side of door reflected the street and the yard but they were like one way mirrors. Whoever was on the other side could see out, but Maddie couldn't see what was on the other side.

Not that it mattered. She knew what was inside. She'd been here often enough. Just not lately, she thought.

Maddie reached inside her suit jacket and took out her id wallet.

She took out the proxima card she kept there and ran it over a section of wall next to the door.

There was a barely audible click and the door slide aside into the door frame. Mattie waited until the familiar mechanical voice spoke.

"Identify," it said. She'd never been able to determine if the voice was male or female not that it mattered, but intellectual games were something she enjoyed.

"Madeline Surefoot. Operative number 27, Internal Secrets Bureau."

There was a two second delay (yes, Maddie counted the elapsed time) then the voice said, "Identity verified. You may enter."

"Thank you." Though it was unnecessary to thank a machine Maddie had always considered politeness a worthwhile human virtue that separated them from the machines, and the beings in unreality who she considered non-human.

After she stepped through the open door it slide closed with a whoosh and a soft thud. Before her was the reception area with it's waterfall in one corner of the wide, carpeted lobby. The waterfall fell into a oval shaped pond bordered by a small forest of dwarf palm tress and tropical ferns and flowering pants.

The variety and splash of color and the bubble of water striking the small pond had always given Maddie a sense of inner peace.

She cringed inside when she saw Rocky Almost was working reception today. He was obviously on the telephone, speaking into his headset, his gray eyes focused on the flat screen monitor in front of him.

She and Rocky had dated for six months, until she discovered he had been living with another woman for over a year even after they began to date. She'd forgiven him, but it still hurt her to her core to see him. Ever since Rocky her trust of the male gender had never been at such a low level as it was now.

She approached the desk just as he ended the call. "Thanks and have a nice day." Rocky pressed a finger against the side of the headset.

Her mouth formed a tight smile as she tried to catch his attention. "Hi, Rocky," she said brightly.

He looked up from his monitor at her but he didn't smile. "Hello, Ms. Surefoot."

The use of her last name hurt Maggie worse than if he'd called her every four letter word in the dictionary. Whatever they had once felt for each was truly dead and gone. It was like they'd never know each other at all.

"I'm here to see my mother," she said, letting the smile fall away from her lips.

"Ok." He glanced at her id badge then placed a clipboard with an excel spreadsheet-style form and a pen attached by a string. There were columns for names, dates and times. He pointed with his index finger to the next empty space on the form. "Name date and time," he said, his tone dull.

"I know the drill," she said, restraining herself from snapping the words out. Given his hard exterior it seemed unlikely he'd be affected in the least anyway.

She completed the form then turned and walked away headed for the corridor than ran down the middle of the first floor. Behind her she heard him say, "Have a nice visit."

Maddie hesitated then rushed away, the knuckles of her right hand white from gripping the strap of her handbag that hung off her right shoulder.

She held back tears and her heart beat hard in her chest. She suppressed her emotions as she hurried down then wide tiled hallway past the recreation room, the theater and the gymnasium. Along the way she met several residents she knew.

Mrs. Campbell, a retired MI6 agent, Mr. Nahan, retired from Kenya's National Security Intelligence Service, and Mr. Yamanta, from Japan's Giant Monster Intelligence Bureau. She nodded at each one as she passed them. Mr. Yamanta had been living here for more than sixty years, but he didn't look a day over sixty himself. Maddie wish she knew the secret to his longevity.

Finally she arrived at her mother's room. She closed her eyes took a deep breath then released it slowly. After wiping her cheeks with the back of her hand she opened her eyes and rapped her knuckles on the door.

"Come in, dahlin,'" she heard her mother's distinctive southern accent come through the door.

Maddie pasted a smile on her face then opened the door. "Hi, Mom."

She froze when she realized her mother wasn't alone. A very elegant man stood next to her cream colored chaise lounger. He had a perfectly trimmed goatee that formed a sharp point on the end of his angular chin. Stuck in one eye socket was a monocle, and he wore a black velvet smoking jacket and perfectly pressed gray slacks. A fire engine red scarf surrounded his thin neck. It was tucked down the front of his jacket.

Her mother looked the same as always. Her dyed black hair was piled atop her head perfectly permed into tight curls. Upon seeing her daughter she leapt to her feet seeming to fly off the lounger, and threw her arms wide and ran at Maddie and wrapped her arms around her and hugged her tightly. Maddie thought about drawing her weapon.

"Maddie! My dahling girl! How long has it been?"

It had been what ten seconds and her mother had already started berating her for not visiting. "Two months, Mom. I'm sorry, I—"

Her mother startled her when she laughed brightly and released her. Her mother's eyes were bright and cheerful and she wore a wide smile on her face. Most importantly her eyes reflected her happiness.

Had her mother been smoking wacky-tabaccy, or was she drunk?

One of Maddie's eyebrows arched. There wasn't the tell-tale smell of marijuana smoke and she hadn't detected liquor on her mothers breath when she hugged her.

Hugged me? Maybe her mother had been assimilated by aliens? It had been known to happen. "Mom? Are you okay?"

It was then she realized her mother was dressed in a beautiful silk kimono that flowed around her body giving her the illusion of floating on air. Her mother laughed again then went to sprawl once again on the chaise lounger again. "No, no, dahling', I'm fine. I'm just in love is all." Her mother waved a hand at her. "Silly girl. Haven't you ever been in love?"

Maddie knew love, but she'd never seen her mother in love. Her father had disappeared when she was a little girl. Seeing her mother this way was a new and strange experience.

"Yeah, Mom, of course, but you haven't…" Maddie hesitated as her face grew warm. "You haven't been in love as long as…" Her voice trailed off. Had her mother loved her father? She had no idea, it wasn't something they'd ever talked about.

"Yes, muh dear daughter. I loved your father very much, but he's not coming back from the fourth dimension." She paused to grin at Maddie. "I'd like you to meet Lord Blacktoe, my fiancée."

The elegant looking man who'd bee silently observing them turned toward Maddie and held out one hand. "Charmed, Ms. Surefoot."

Maddie took his hand in hers and cringed inside. It was like shaking the tail of a dead fish.

"Pleased to meet you, Lord Blacktoe, so you wish to marry my mother?"

"Yes, Ms. Surefoot, I'm madly in love." Was he kidding? It was like he'd just told her he preferred marmalade on his toast.

Maddie offered him a tight smile then turned toward her mother. "Mother, I'm afraid I'm not here for a social call. There has been some trouble I need to talk to you about." She indicated Lord Blacktoe with a slight nod. "In private."

"Oh, poo, poo, dahling', Alfie is MI6. Retired, o' course. He's cleared to the highest level. Something' he calls the Official Secrets Act says if he tells anyone the Brits have to kill him. I'm shore he won't tell anyone. " Her mother batted her eyes at Lord Blacktoe. "Isn't that right, Alfie?"

The man's expression remained stoic he nodded his head ever so slightly, after his eyes had flitted between them. Did his expression ever change even when he was…Maddie pushed away the unimaginable image before it took hold in her mind. She shuddered and wanted to roll her eyes but managed not stop herself.

"Sure, Mom, no problem. Anyway, we found this big red shoe and—"

"The giant," her mother interrupted her. As if she were a balloon she sagged into the cushions of the lounger and her features went slack as all color drained from her cheeks. "He's back," she whispered.

Maddie crossed her arms over her chest. "That's what we thought, until intelligence confirmed the bridge to unreality was still closed. There have been no other intrusions. At least that we know of."

Her mother's smooth forehead wrinkled. Sometimes Maddie thought with all the surgery her mother was starting to look younger than she did. "Then it has to be Jack," said her mother.

"Who?" Maddie's heart rate increased.

Her mother looked into her eyes, her features were taunt and her eyes seemed to bore into her daughters. "Jack, dear. Of Jack and the Beanstalk."

Maddie steered her Aston Martin DB9 into an empty parking stall that surrounded Beanstalk Park. The site where the beanstalk had been chopped down over fifty years ago was now a national monument surrounded by a park complete with picnic tables, a children's playground, and barbecue pits. It was a favorite spot for weekend family outings.

Since today was Saturday there were a myriad of Volvo station wagons and minivans occupying every other parking stall in the lot. Maddie's tricked out sports car was going to stick out like a frog in an onion field.

Maddie turned off the engine and got out. She kept her dark sunglasses on as she strolled toward the thirty yard wide stump. The stump was all that remained of the once awe inspiring beanstalk that ended in unreality.

There was a sign between two steel posts embedded deep into the grass in front of the stump. The sign gave a short history of the stump and the beanstalk, leaving out the important secret details of how it had been cut down and who had done the task.

Maddie's mother had used a laser gun to cut the stalk down. Fortunately the area where the great stalk had fallen had been mostly uninhabited so no one was hurt when it crashed to Earth. A few cows, some sheep, and a few rabbits, had been crushed, and seismographs around the world had registered six points on the Richter scale, but the property damage had been minimal. The ISB had paid off anyone who submitted a claim, a fact even Congress didn't know about. Black ops money was way off the books, and an operation like that cost huge amounts of cash.

Maddie sauntered up to the fence guarded the stump so the children wouldn't climb it and to prevent teenagers from carving their initials into the green stalk. Kids. Maddie shook her head and smiled to herself.

Her mother explained that the Jack who'd managed to transport the red shoe wasn't the original Jack. Apparently original Jack had been a very busy boy in unreality.

He had dated most of the female children of the old-woman-who- lived-in-a-shoe-who-had-so-many-children-she-didn't-know-what-to-do and the giant. She and the giant had sired several hundred children.

Before he left unreality, Jack, had fathered a lot of children. Apparently, the male children were all named Jack Junior. As stupid as it sounded it made sense when you had so many children you didn't know what to name them.

Maddie scanned the park from where she stood by the fence. Children, dogs, mom's and dad's, everyone enjoying the sunny warm weather. Maddie had to push away the sadness that gripped her. Her family had never enjoyed simple pleasures like a day the park. Her family had too often been apart separated by continents or dimensions or where ever the latest secret mission took them.

She'd never had any intention but to join the family business when she was old enough. Her mother once explained that being a spy was in the blood. Secret agent work was a family tradition going to back to the days when an Italian ancestor worked uncover as a Roman agent. Maximus Gallus Surefoot accompanied the Hannibal expedition. He sabotaged Hannibal's plans to conquer the Roman empire.

Maddie frowned as her eyes settled on a man across the park.   Near a stand of pine trees. He looked out of place. He was short, in fact so short, she suspected he was a little person (she decided she wouldn't mention it). He wore a black and white pinstriped suit and on his head he wore a straw hat titled to one side at a cocky angle. Most notably he was alone, like her.

She wondered what he was doing here in the park. His eyes were covered by dark sunglasses and he appeared to be studying her. The most direct approach seemed the most practical.

She approached the little man her eyes warily flitting side to side looking for threats. The man didn't move. She continued when there were no obvious threats.

"Hello," she said as she came up to him.

"Hello, Operative 27." His voice had a surprisingly deep baritone quality to it.

Her eyes narrowed. "Do I know you?"

The corners of his curled. "No. But Chief Wallup does. She sent me."

Maddie's stomach muscles tightened. Obviously Barb didn't want to tell her about this contact. "Oh? Who are you then?"

"I'm with R&D." He paused, turned around and started to walk into the trees. "Follow me. I have something to show you."

Maddie hesitated. Walking into an unknown forest with a man she didn't know was reckless if not irresponsible. As a precaution Maddie reached into her suit jacket and pulled out her ASP semi-automatic pistol. She didn't want to shoot anyone but she would if cornered. The ASP was a good weapon for close quarters like this forest of trees.

The little man was quick so she was breathing hard when she arrived in the clearing. What she saw made her breath catch in her throat and she froze where she stood.

A two story balloon floated above the mashed down grass in the clearing. It was tethered to the ground by ropes tied to wooden stakes pounded into the ground. Red, yellow and blue stripes covered the balloon.

The air was thick with the smell of rotting leaves and cut grass.

"Operative 27, come over here."

Maddie took in a breath and looked in the direction of the man's voice. Beside the balloon stood the man. He'd doffed his sunglasses revealing sapphire blue eyes.

"What's the balloon for?" Maddie asked as she holstered her gun beneath her jacket.

"I'm going to take you to unreality in this balloon." Maddie looked at him the surprise registering on her face. The man held out a business card.

Maddie took it and read his name was Mike Oz, PhD, Mac, Eng. "So you're the Wizard of Oz?" Maddie smirked. "Nice try, pal."

The little man laughed. "No, of course not. I'm a scientist and I'm going to take you to unreality in this balloon."

Maddie eyed Dr. Oz with one eyebrow cocked. She'd seen a lot of strange things, a balloon that would take her to unreality wasn't outside the realm of possibility.

"I thought the portal between reality and unreality wasn't accessible."

Dr. Oz shrugged. "It isn't, for most people."

"Do you have a permit?" Permits were required to travel to unreality. Maddie had never seen one but she knew it was a requirement.

"Uhhh…not exactly."

"Not exactly, huh? That's what I thought." Maddie turned to walk away. "I'm so outta here."

"Hold on, Ms. Surefoot." Maddie stopped. "Chief Wallup wants you to go. That's why she sent me to see you. It's dangerous, against the rules, and filled with adventure. Most importantly if we do this its very likely we'll save the world."

Maddie spun around a wide smile pasted to her tanned features.

"Now that's my kind of mission. Let's get this balloon in the air."

###

After three hours of flying time they arrived in unreality. The balloon floated on the warm air. Giant birds, with what looked like forty foot wing spans, floated along side them their wings spread in order to ride the updrafts.

Maddie spotted the giant's castle first on the horizon the twin stone towers piercing the puffy white clouds.

The same birds that now floated in the air around them had constructed nests along the castle walls and some sections of wall had collapsed reminiscent of a child that had lost baby teeth sporadically.

Had something happened to the giant?

They soon arrived at the castle and Dr. Oz managed to find a safe place to land amongst the stones that fell and landed haphazardly along the base of the castle walls. The castle and the surrounding area looked deserted.

The forest had encroached the park-like area that bordered the castle land, and the grass had grown waist high in sections.

What bothered Maddie was evidence of a battle. Large sections of grass had been burned black and some trees in the nearby forest were charred, some having collapsed, or the tree trunks were shattered before they were blown apart.

Who in unreality had the nerve and the firepower to go up against the giant?

What she didn't realize was the grounds were imbedded with sensors and their arrival had been noted.

Half an hour later a green army jeep broke from the forest.

Three men rode in the vehicle with one man standing in the bed of the jeep manning a machine gun. Maddie watched their approach with trepidation. Who's army were these guys with?

All of the men wore reflective aviator glasses and the passenger had an unlit cigar between his teeth. The men's rippling biceps were bare, tanned and covered in scars.

The passenger had the butt of an automatic rifle resting on his thigh the barrel pointed to the sky.

"Hey, there, little lady," said the passenger over the squeal of the jeeps brakes as it stopped in front of them.

Maddie crossed her arms over her chest and shifted her weight to her left leg. "Name's ISB Operative Madeline Surefoot, not little lady." She reached into her pocket and pulled out her identification wallet and flashed her credentials.

The man chuckled and removed his sunglasses to reveal a warm brown eyes a woman could get lost in. "Sorry, Ms. Surefoot, name's Jack. I'm in charge of this military zone."

Maddie arched an eyebrow. "Really? You're Jack? Well, then, Jack, tell me what's happened here."

The smile dissipated from Jack's rugged features. "War. Death. Blood."

"Sorry? War? With whom?"

Jack got out of the jeep. Maddie was impressed. He was over six feet tall with a wide chest and muscular arms. He moved with the confidence and strength of someone who could handle himself. He threw the cigar to the ground then crushed it under his boot heel. "You've heard of the old woman who—"

"Yes. I know who she is. What about her?" Maddie was growing impatient. Barb wanted her in unreality for a reason, and it wasn't to play footsie with some soldier boy, as appealing as that might be. Jack was clearly handsome and just the type that would break her heart.

The guy probably had hot and cold running blondes back at base camp.

Jack eyed her with a sly grin on his lips. "My grandmother is leading the defense of unreality."

"Revolution? Against what? Fairy's and goblins?"

"Not exactly. You see—" The stone wall behind them exploded raining them with bits of rock and mortar. Smoke and dust filled Maddie's nose and mouth

"Com'on!" yelled Jack. "We have to go."

He jumped into the jeep while the man with the machine gun began firing sporadically into the forest.

Maddie ran to the jeep with Dr. Oz close behind her.

Jack motioned for her to sit in his lap and Dr. Oz to climb into the back. Maddie considered protesting but another explosion to her right made up her mind. She sat across his lap and he wrapped one arm around her waist to keep from falling as the jeep jerked and started to drive in a zigzag pattern across the open park land. Maddie locked her arms around Jack's neck and held on as the jeep swayed side to side and bounced across the open field.

The drivers features were grim and his arms were stiff with tension as he struggled to keep the jeep from rolling over due to the sudden increase in weight.

An explosion near the front left bumper sprayed them with dirt. The driver made a sharp turn to the right to avoid the crater created by whatever ordinance the enemy was using. Maddie felt like she'd lose her lunch. She tasted bile at the back of her throat.

The driver drove like a man possessed (which is entirely possible in unreality) until they rounded a cliff. With a wall between them the explosions stopped but the driver kept zigzagging.

After twenty minutes they arrived an encampment surrounded by guard towers on the four corners.

Teams of men and women stood in the guard towers scanning the plains that ran away toward the granite cliff they'd left behind them. The jeep pulled up to a guard house and gate and came to a stop, the brakes squeaking loudly.

"Sergeant Jack Bean, Recon Unit 6." He indicated Maddie with a nod. "This is ISB Operative Surefoot. The guy in the back is Dr. Oz, ISB R&D."

The guard nodded. "Thank you, Sergeant. You may pass."

Maddie started when she heard the familiar sound of a bolt being cocked on a fifty caliber machine from somewhere above them.

She glanced at Jack. He offered a twisted smile. "The war hasn't been going too well. Creates itchy trigger fingers," he explained simply before the jeep bounced beneath them and they roared into the compound.

They stopped in front of a forest green canvas tent. Maddie extracted herself from Jack's lap and everyone piled out.

Jack faced his three soldiers. "You guys go have a shower and get some hot chow. Meet me back here at 1900 hours."

"Will do, Sarge," said the driver. The other two men merely nodded their expression unreadable.

Jack turned toward Maddie and Dr. Oz. "I'll take you to see my grandmother."

Maddie nodded and attempted to smooth her rumpled suit with her hands. A few stray hairs fell across her eyes. She blew them away only to see them fall back. She stole a glance at Oz and saw he was trembling, badly shaken by the wild ride.

She patted his shoulder. He looked at her and she smiled at him. "That's what field work is like pretty much all the time. Fun, huh?"

Oz cleared his throat. "Yeah. Fun."

Jack snorted obviously amused by Dr. Oz's reaction. "The general is in this tent," he said, nodding toward the tent the jeep was parked in front of.

They followed Jack inside the tent to find a gray haired woman with the weathered features of someone who'd spent too much time in the sun. The lines on her face reminded Maddie of aged leather. The old woman was seated behind a large ornate oak desk. Her brown eyes looked up from the paper she'd been reading when they entered. When her eyes settled on Jack her weathered features broke into a wide smile. She got up and moved quickly around the desk. She wrapped her arms around Jack and hugged him to her.

After several seconds they broke their hug and she took a step back and gripped his arms with gnarled hands. She gazed into his eyes.

"I heard there was an attack?"

Jack grinned. "No, worries, Gran. Pete got us outta there okay. He's one heck of a driver."

She released Jack from her grip and dropped her arms to her sides. The smile on her face disappeared, only to be replaced by a deep frown.

"Yes, but it means they're close. Too close." She walked around her desk and sat down. "Who are they?"

Jack chuckled. "Sorry. This is ISB Operative Surefoot and Dr. Oz. We found them at Rednose's castle and decided not to leave them to the hostiles."

"For which I and Dr. Oz are very grateful," said Maddie. "General, I must know, what is going on?"

The general gazed at Maddie with dead eyes and her features darkened. "Why were you sent to unreality?"

"With respect, General, I believe I asked a question."

The general leaned forward in her chair and laid her arms flat on the desk. "We are at war with the giants and others, and we don't have a lot of time. Now tell me, why are you here?"

Giants? Plural. There were more than one of them? Oh well, in for a buck in for twenty. "Because of a red shoe that landed in reality."

Maddie frowned. "But what about Rednose? He's a giant."

The general's features softened and her eyes became bright with tears. "He died. When my husband refused to join in with their war they killed him…" Her voice trailed off and she wiped at her eyes with the sleeve of her uniform shirt. Maddie had seen such pain before and decided she'd drop the obviously painful subject.

She cleared her throat and shifted her gaze to Jack. "Is the shoe drop your doing, Sergeant?"

He nodded his mouth a grim line.

The general sighed and eased back in her chair. "We're losing the war, and Jack thought your world might be willing to help."

"What makes you think that?" Maddie frowned at Jack. He grinned sheepishly and her heart fluttered. He was way too handsome for his own good.

"Because, Operative Surefoot, if we lose, your world will be next."

***

Maddie was excited when the general asked Maddie to work with Jack on strategies and plans for counter attack. It would give her chance to know him better.

They stood side by side looking over a waist high table made form sawhorses and plywood. A large map of the battle fields had been spread out on the table and blue and red pins had been used to indicate the coordinates of both sides. Maddie's frown grew deeper the longer she stared at it and realized what it was telling her.

The enemy had broken through their defensive lines in several places. This had resulted in retreating battles between the army of the shoe and the giants and their allies the dwarfs (yes, the irony is not lost on me) and the ogres. Most of the fairytale creatures were with them. A entire village of cookie people and pie makers had declared themselves neutral. So far the enemy had honored their neutrality, but Maddie knew it was only a matter of time before they too were drawn into the war.

Jack stood beside her smelling of soap and cigar smoke. Right now an unlit cigar stuck out from between his gritted teeth. <u>At least he washed.</u> "So what do ya think?" he said.

"You guys are pretty much screwed."

Jack grunted. "Yeah. I know. Any ideas?"

"You mean other than heading for the hills?" She shook her head and emitted a sharp laugh. "But since your pretty much surrounded and the enemy is closing in that ship has sailed."

"So we surrender and hope they don't execute us?"

"Nope. We ask Dr. Oz to build us some weapons. Non-lethal weapons."

She glanced at Jack and saw the arrogant smile had faded and his features had paled. Good, she thought, I threw him a curve ball.

She turned to face him. "Non-lethal weapons will preserve the balance in unreality. If the giants and ogres are all gone then who will rise up and take over?" She arched an eyebrow. "You? The general? The wild unicorns?" Her eyes narrowed. "Or maybe the wizards? We certainly don't want the wizards to take control. That would be very bad and for your world and mine."

Jack's eyes narrowed and he stroked his stubble covered chin with strong fingers. He looked so handsome she had to stop herself from shivering. "I see what you mean." He dropped his hand to his side, his palm now resting off the butt of his pistol in the holster around his narrow waist.

"But can Dr. Oz build enough weapons, fast enough to turn the tide of, " with his left hand he swept an arc over the map, "this."

Maddie nodded grimly. "I think we have a month. Dr. Oz can and will do it." Her voice lowered to a whisper. "Or we all die."

***

Maddie rubbed the eye pieces of her gas mask before she stole a look over the wall of sandbags. There they were. The giants were moving across the open field toward their position. The looked warily and slapped their hairy palms with their tree sized wooden clubs.

In the last month Dr. Oz had constructed several new classes of weapons for the locals that had taken out several hundred giants and ogres. The fairies and shoe elves had worked night and day to turn out non-lethal bubble guns, and shock cannons, and giggle grenades. These weapons had turned the tide of war in their favor. Maddie was relieved the enemy hadn't changed tactics when the new weapons were deployed and continued to be dependant on their brute force alone.

All that remained of the giants, dwarfs, and ogres army were five giants. The rest of their army had been incapacitated and captured. It was up to her and Jack to take out these last few.

Maddie slipped down once again behind the wall and reached for the box of giggle grenades. She glanced at Jack in his gas mask and they shared an awkward smile.

These giants were going to get a big surprise when they got within range. The incoming giants were causing the ground to tremble beneath the defenders. The earth shook more violently with each deep thud of their massive boot steps as they drew ever closer.

Finally, when Maddie thought they were close enough, she issued the order her troops had been waiting for with a loud yell. "Now!"

She stood up with a grenade in her right hand, Jack did the same. They each pulled the pin, counted to three, then threw the grenades into the path of the oncoming giants. They dropped down once again behind the sandbags and covered their heads with their arms.

There was a loud bang and the invisible gas dispersed. Maddie heard the giants coughing and the first giggles started. Soon they were laughing uncontrollably. After ten minutes elapsed she heard the five giants fall with thuds so loud she had to cover her ears, her teeth chattered, and the impact made her heart skip a beat.

Maddie began to laugh herself as did Jack. She and Jack had become close and for the first time in along time it seemed she could trust a man again.

Jack turned out to be a kind and gentle man with great passion, and he was a good kisser. But if he was going to win her heart he would have to give up the cigars and shave once in awhile. The latter not too often, of course, she kind of enjoyed the feeling of his stubble on her skin.

After the mop up crews had these remaining giant's secured, and locked in the holding pen to await trial for crimes against unreality, Maddie met with General She-Had-So-Many-Children-She-Didn't-Know-What-To-Do.

They each had a cup of warm mint tea in front of them. "So, my dear, when are you going back?"

"Back?" Maddie sipped her tea.

The general shrugged. "To reality. To your job. Your old life."

Maddie shook her head. "I think I'll stick around for a while."

The general arched one eyebrow. "Oh? Is it my grandson?"

Maddie chuckled. "Yes, partially. But I don't think these giants were alone. I think someone helped them, or incited them.

They seem to be puppets of a greater power."

"You may be right." The general's tired eyes dropped to peer at her tea cup. A small smile drifted across her pale lips. "I was hoping you'd make an honest man of my grandson."

Maddie lifted her cup to her lips and peered at the old woman over the rim. Before she took another sip she said, "That could be a distinct possibility.

Hard to believe this had all started with one red shoe. Maddie was certain Barb would understand her reasons for staying. She only hoped her mother would.

Shoeless Moe

THE DAY SHE CALLED me I sat at my cigarette scarred desk in the dimly lit news room with nothing to write about. The city editor had just killed my series about the mob's control of the unions. The editor said they were poorly written pieces. But I knew the real reason was he was getting pressure from the boy's downtown. The mob was throwing a lot of green around these days, and the politico types had become the mob's lap dogs.

She told me her name was Old Woman and that she lost a shoe, a really big shoe. Old Woman claimed she lived in the shoe with so many kids she didn't know what to do.

A fact that would lead to her death, and my arrest for her murder.

My name's Rumplestiltskin. I'm a reporter for Big City Bugle newspaper, and my beat is the night desk.

Like every dame in Big City I knew right away she was working an angle. Red headed dames are the trickiest ones. I called up her picture up on the worldwide web as we talked. I saw a woman with hair the color of carrots, so her intentions were immediately clear. And I'm a confirmed blond man, but redheads and brunettes are okay by me.

From the moment I heard her sweet talk a sour feeling grew deep in my gut. But my weakness for the fairer sex too often gets me in deep.

We agreed to meet on the wrong side of the tracks, out near the Moldy Projects, named after Rusk Moldy, the crooked developer. As it usually does in Big City it was raining hard by the time I got there.

I had the collar of my trench coat pulled up tight around my pointed ears, and shivered when a cold raindrop fell off the brim of my gray felt fedora to run down my neck. That was when I spotted her standing in the yellow light of a street lamp smoking a long cigarette. I licked my lips, and for the millionth time this week, suppressed the urge to bum a smoke. I always pick the lousiest times to give up a perfectly good vice.

Tall and willowy, her makeup heavy, so thick in fact it looked like it had been applied with a pallet knife. Her full lips were painted red, and her pea green eye shadow emphasized her almond shaped eyes. As I got closer I realized she was much older than she looked from a distance. But then I'm a four hundred year old troll so who am I to call the witches cauldron black?

As I stepped from the thick shadows into the pale light of the street lamp her emerald eyes smiled at the same time as her sensual mouth. Good thing. If I had thought this was a trap I would have used the .38 I kept in the shoulder holster hidden beneath my gray trench coat. The one the cops don't know about.

I hadn't shaved in a coupla days, and my breath probably reeked of the shot of cheap whiskey I drank before leaving the office, but hey in my line of work I'm what's referred to as the diamond-in-the-rough.

When Mrs. Woman telephoned she told me her giant shoe had disappeared. When I asked her what she meant by disappeared she explained she'd been on a date with a man and when she came back it wasn't where she left it.

Now in Big City a missing shoe isn't news, unless its five stories high, and her date is with Milo Grimm, Capo for the Grimm Brothers mob. This dame had gotten my attention.

The Grimm's control the rackets on the west aide. Every speakeasy, gin joint, pimp, and gambling den pays the Grimm's protection money. Any who refuse disappear into Never Never Land. I've known a few city editors who I often wished would double cross the Grimm's so they'd disappear, but then who'd be stupid enough to cross the Grimm's?

My well-tuned reporter seventh sense told me the dame was gonna make one heck of a story, and I wanted in on the ground floor.

"Hey, doll," I kept my tone light. My let's-be-friends mode was set on charming.

She regarded me coolly as I watched rain drip off the edge of her wide brimmed hat. One perfectly plucked eyebrow arched on her pale forehead. Under her gaze I felt the familiar twinge in that nice-ta-meet-ya place.

"You Rumplestiltskin?" Naturally she already knew who I was, or she wouldn't have been standing under this street lamp. Playing dumb was a way of life in the underbelly of the Big City. Always force the other guy to show his hole card first. She is a clever gal this one.

"Yes, ma'am." I grinned.

Her eyes narrowed and she took a drag on her cigarette, held it for a second or two, then blew the smoke in my face. I blinked and coughed. "Want one?" Evidently she recognized a reformed nicotine addict when she saw one.

"No. Thanks." I wiped the tear from my left eye with the back of one hand.

Her voice was husky with an extra layer of sexy. "So, Mr. Rumplestiltskin, can you help me find my lost shoe?"

"Sure," I nodded, "I know a few people in this town. I'm pretty certain someone'll know who stole a size way-too-big-for-us-normals shoe." I shrugged. "I mean who wants a giant shoe?

Her pencil thin eyebrows shot up. "A woman with too many children, perhaps?" There was an amused edge in her tone.

I nodded and stuffed my hands in the pockets of my trench coat. "Yeah. I know a little about rug rats."

"Really? You don't look like the child-friendly type to me."

I grinned. "I wasn't always a Big City byline ya know." Her sensuous mouth broke into a pleasant smile then she laughed brightly.

How do ya like that? I made a funny, even though I didn't mean to be funny.

Now boyo, I cautioned myself, don't let her flattery cause your head to swell to the size of your ego. You're not that funny. I looked around. "So where was this shoe when it went missing?"

She shook her head. "I said it disappeared, remember?"

"Yeah. Sorry. Is there a difference?"

She ignored my question. "Follow me." She wiggled an index finger to beckon me to walk with her out of the protection of the street lamp and into the inky darkness.

When I followed her into the blackness outside the circle of light of the street lamp it was as if I'd suddenly gone blind. I couldn't see even my hand, or anything else, in front of my face. The world disappeared in black ink. She instructed me to look straight ahead and avoid looking back at the light, so my eyes would adjust to the darkness. Old said she wanted me to see something. Something important.

As we stood side-by-side I heard her breathing and smelled her cheesecake scented perfume. I've never enjoyed sweet desserts, even feminine ones. They rot your teeth and your mind at the same time, and usually they steal your wallet before you wake up in the morning.

After about five minutes of silence, the only sound the pounding of rain off the cracked and oily pavement, my eyesight had adjusted enough so I could make out two abandoned brick walkups. Between them was a large gap. Could this be where the giant shoe once stood?

If it was then this thing had left one colossal footprint. I would hate to meet the owner of a shoe that big. I frowned. If she lived in one giant sized shoe I wondered where the other half of the pair was.

My answer was a sharp blow to the back of the head and the world disappeared.

* * *

When I woke it was morning. I opened my eyes looking into a face only a bulldog would love. Lieutenant Manny "Mother" Goose of Big City PD's Homicide Division glowered at me from under the brim of his chocolate brown fedora. He gnawed at his unlit cigar that hung from the side of the slash in the middle of his jowly mug, I loosely refer to as a mouth. Mother and I gave up smoking on the same day. It wasn't a good day. I hoped today would be better, but somehow I doubted it.

"Rump, you alive?"

"Unless you're the devil welcoming me to hell, yeah I'm alive." My voice sounded like sandpaper. When his expression didn't change I added, "What happened?"

I groaned when I tried to raise my head and pain shot across my forehead and my guts twisted. I was going to vomit for sure. I eased my head back to the ground and closed my eyes and waited for the nausea to pass.

"Somebody knocked your noodle into next week," said Mother.

My eyes fluttered open and I blinked to clear the fog in my head. "Now I know why you're the detective and I'm the lowly reporter."

As my vision cleared I saw the sky above was gray with billowing, angry clouds, but at least it wasn't raining. Yet.

I managed to raise to myself to my elbows as Mother stepped back, his thumbs hooked off the pockets of the vest under his cheap wool suit jacket. He turned his back to me to face the abandoned buildings.

My eyes narrowed as I studied my surroundings. The two abandoned brick walkups were still there, rust-colored bricks covered with black mold. Between them was the largest footprint I'd ever seen. Old Woman clearly wasn't exaggerating.

The shoe had to be at least a size four hundred, triple E.

"Where's the dame?" I asked.

Mother glanced over his shoulder at me and nodded to a spot beside me surrounded by banana-yellow caution tape. In the middle of the tape was a puddle of goo. "That's what's left," he said casually.

My eyes went wide and I froze. "What happened?"

"Somebody slimed her," he said simply.

"I can see that, Mother, but who and why?"

"We're not sure why yet, but we suspect it was a lovers spat, or maybe an attempted rape." He paused and swung round to face me.

"You and I've known each other a long time, eh Rump?"

I nodded slowly. I didn't like where he was going with this line of questioning. "Yeah. Sure, Mother you and I go way back. We had some good times and a few giggles."

Mother shrugged and sighed. "Yeah. Good times." His words trailed off. Suddenly his eyes locked on mine. "Listen, Rump I have my orders. People farther up the food chain smell blood. I'm sure you understand."

My mouth twisted in a sardonic grin. "I'm under arrest, right?"

Mother winced like he'd sucked on a lemon and nodded.

I sat up feeling suddenly better. My headache was nearly gone and the knot in my stomach had eased. It all made sense. A for-show arrest, then Mother would vouch for me, and I'd be back at my desk before noon writing the story of the missing giant shoe, the mobster romance gone sour, and the cheesecake scented puddle of goo. What a story this was gonna be.

"I know what you're thinkin', Rump but it's not gonna be that simple," Mother's mouth became a grim line.

I looked at him and frowned. "What do you mean? It's ridiculous to think I'd kill a dame I just met." I walked toward the gap where the giant shoe print was clearly visible in the light brown soil and waved my arm at it to emphasize my point. "I wouldn't kill a woman I hated, never mind some gal I just met. And I only met her because she called me and asked me to meet her here." I scowled at him. Now I was plain old mad. This was the biggest injustice since that idiot baked blackbirds in a pie.

"I think you better hold on, Rump and stop talking. I have to read you your rights so you shouldn't say nothin' without a legal eagle present."

I stared at Mother and realized he was serious. I felt my face grow flush with anger. "You can't be serious about charging me?"

Ignoring me, as if I were a common criminal, Mother pulled back one side of my suit jacket and pulled my .38 from my shoulder holster as he began to recite my rights. "Rumplestiltskin, you have the right…"

I didn't listen to the rest. I knew it by heart anyway. Working the night beat you see a lot of arrests. I could never figure out why criminals always seem to work at night. Especially murderers. What's wrong with murdering someone in the afternoon, or before lunch? At least then you'd have the rest of the day to do what you want.

But nope, not in Big City. In Big City murders happen after sunset.

I glanced at the goo. She may have been old, but she was a looker. Mother was right about two things; I just met the Old Woman who lived in a shoe, and I was gonna miss her.

I narrowed my eyes to slits. There was something very wrong with all this.

"Do you understand these rights as I have explained them?" finished Mother in the familiar bland monotone he used for all his arrests.

"Yeah, sure. Whatever. But, Mother explain this to me, how do you know this goo is her goo?" I indicated the gelatinous substance behind the yellow tape with a slight nod of my head. I sniffed the air. "And I smell Cinnamon not cheesecake." I felt a growing sense of excitement. I was onto something and my reporter instincts were in high gear.

Mother looked at me as if I'd grown two heads. The cheesecake part is probably a little over the top.

"The lab boys ran some tests," Mother shrugged his wide shoulders. He pulled his handcuffs from the leather holder on his belt and came toward me. "Put both hands on your head, then place one hand behind your back."

When Mother came up behind me to snap the handcuffs round my wrists I smelled his warm garlic breath then I heard him whisper, "Run."

I had a split second to decide if I should. Naturally, I always follow whispered instructions so I elbowed Mother in the gut. He grunted and I took off running across the gap between the buildings.

I've never been a runner so before I went fifty feet I was breathing hard and sweat poured down my leathery face. My mouth felt like it was crammed full of cotton balls.

I heard a voice behind me that wasn't Mother's yell for me to stop or he'd shoot. I didn't stop and I didn't look back. What I did do was will my rubbery legs to carry me faster and faster.

The distinct sound of a pistol hammer being cocked echoed off the buildings on either side of me. I knew I was seconds away from death by .38 police special. I kept my feet moving. but it was like I was running underwater, because I seemed to be going slower and slower.

I almost made it to the far edge of the buildings, where I'd be able to take cover, when a shot rang out. I tripped and fell face first hard into the mud.

I thought at first I was hit, but there wasn't any pain so I knew he'd missed.

"Rump! Move your butt!" I raised my head and wiped away the mud from my eyes. When I was able to see again I looked back and saw Mother had his gun out and was urging me on with it. I froze when I saw the trial of smoke coming from the barrel and the unmoving uniformed cop lying face down in front of him.

I realized Mother had set me up as a cop killer. Now every cop in Big City would be gunning for me. I wasn't wanted dead or alive, I was wanted sooo dead. Et tu, Mother?

* * *

Someone had bought off the locals to make sure I was edited out of the picture. But why kill the girl? And why steal a big shoe? This wasn't making a lot of sense.

I ran up the steps of the brownstone tenement building of the Van Allen Belt working class neighborhood taking two stairs at a time. I was breathing hard as I stood outside apartment 4C.

Along the way here I had stopped in City Park to wash the mud off as best I could in the public restroom. Three junkies slept peacefully in the stalls when I was running water in the sink. The towel dispenser had stood empty for over twenty years so I was forced to cup water in my palms and scoop it to wash the mud off my clothes and face. The water reeked of rust and decay. Like everything else in this rot infested town the water had even turned on me.

My only hope now was to get out of Big City. And my secretary Cindy Charming was the only hole card left to play. After all she owed me.

I helped her escape the Prince's castle in the bad old days, when the heavy drinking prince had threatened to murder her, and brought her to Big City.

I rapped on the door. The sound echoed down the long hallway.

In less than a minute the door opened a crack. The steel chain was visible across the opening. One inquisitive azure eye peered at me.

"Mr. Rumplestiltskin is that you?" Cindy stepped back and the chain rattled against the doorframe then the door swung open. Cindy wore a slip-over-your-head, floor-length powder blue housecoat that accented her honey blonde hair. The housecoat was closed up to her slender neck.

I never had romantic designs on Cindy. She was young when I brought her here and I considered her my little sister. When we first arrived in Big City I worried her innocence might be corrupted by the dirt and squalor all around us. But she remained the one good person I knew in this town.

I walked in the apartment and closed the door behind me with a thump.

Cindy's apartment matched her personality. A pink throw rug sat under a pine coffee table in front of a pure white sofa. Mustard yellow curtains framed the windows overlooking the street below. A dozen red roses rested in a crystal vase on an end table to the left of the sofa. Their fragrance filled the room.

I looked down at my clothes and hands and realized I better stay right here by the door.

There was no way I was going to track mud on her perfect domestic tranquility.

"Mr. Rumplestiltskin what's happened to you?" Cindy left the room momentarily and came back with a towel.

I thanked her and began to dry my face, hands and hair. "We have to get out of town." Her eyes were wide. "Today, Cindy. We have to leave."

She looked at me dumbfounded as if I were speaking a foreign language. "Cindy, if we don't leave today I will die. Do you understand?"

She nodded and her brow furrowed. "Yes, I do but I'm not leaving."

My jaw dropped and I gapped at her. "What are you talking about? Didn't you hear what I said?"

Cindy nodded grimly. "Yes, as I said already I understand but you're on your own. I'm staying." The determination in her tone made me wonder what happened to Cindy Charming, my little sister, and who was this woman standing before me.

"Cindy, what's the matter with you?"

"Nothing. I have a benefactor. He takes care of me."

A benefactor? My gut twisted. Someone had taken advantage of this sweet young girl and corrupted her. 'Who is it?" I asked between gritted teeth.

"Milo Grimm," she said confidently. She crossed her arms over her chest and turned her back on me. "He told me he was going to set you up for a murder rap because he was hurt by the lies you wrote in the newspaper about his business."

I couldn't believe what I was hearing. "But, Cindy Milo Grimm is a mobster, a criminal. He's using you."

She sniffed. "He said you'd say that." Cindy whirled to face me, her normally gentle features were marred by a scowl. "Just because someone's in the bar business everyone assumes they're mobbed up.

"Milo thought about paying you off, but I told him not to. I know you too well. You're a troll with principals." She scoffed. "Principals that'll land you in the gas chamber."

I let out an exasperated grunt like I'd just been punched in the gut. "Cindy, I thought we loved each other."

Someone pounded on the door interrupting us. We looked at each other. "Are you expecting someone else?" She shook her head.

"See who it is and I'll hide in the bathroom." I hurried to the bathroom and closed the door behind me. I climbed into the bathtub and pulled the shower curtain across.

Unlike my bathroom that hadn't been cleaned in five months hers smelled of lavender and Ivory soap.

I listened intently. I heard her soft tone speaking, not the exact words just a murmur. Then suddenly there were angry words and the thump, thump of pounding feet then the bathroom flew open and thudded against the wall cracking the plaster.

"Rump? It's Mother. You can come out now. It's all over."

I slid the shower curtain aside and saw Mother in his protective vest with his gun in his right hand. He wore a silly grin on his face.

"Did you get him?"

"Yeah," Mother nodded. "Found Milo hiding in a secret passageway in the lady's bedroom." He stuffed his gun back in his shoulder holster then accompanied me to the living room.

Upon entering the room I discovered Cindy and Milo seated side by side on the sofa glaring at the two uniforms standing over them. They weren't going to say anything more, at least not until they met with their lawyer, and probably not even then. We had plenty of Cindy on tape to convict them both for racketeering and conspiracy. It was enough to send them both up the river for long stretches.

I frowned. "Something I don't get, Mother. How do Old Woman and the disappearing giant shoe fit into this?"

Mother laughed. "They don't. We found Old Woman's husband. The shoe is his. When he left town some years back, he left one shoe behind for good luck. Old woman who has so many children knew exactly what to do, she moved her kids into it."

"So who's her husband?"

Mother grinned. "He plays baseball for the Neverland Giants. They call him Shoeless Moe. His real name is Moe Fofum."

I shook my head and chuckled. "I get it. Moe's a giant."

Mother nodded. "Yup, 'bout as big as they get. His nickname's shoeless because he only wears one shoe when he plays. He came home to retrieve the other one. He told me the kids moved out of the shoe years ago, but his wife loved living in it. A lot more room in a giant shoe that a one bedroom apartment these days."

"You spoke to him?"

Mother nodded. "Yeah. Heck of a nice guy for a giant."

"And I assume Old Woman's not dead," I paused, "but what about the goo?"

He shook his head. "Hair gel. Moe wears the stuff his sponsor gives him. Practically bathes in it."

I chuckled and nodded then glanced at Cindy. She avoided looking at me.

I may never write the story about all this. There is just so much pain and heartbreak one reporter can take after another day on the night beat —

— the night beat in Big City.

About the Author

International selling author, Russ Crossley writes romance under the name R.G. Hart, mystery/suspense under the name R.G. Crossley, and science fiction and fantasy under his own. This year there will be re-issues the romantic comedies, Bachelorette: Zombie Edition by Champagne Books, and Antique Virgin by 53rd Street Publishing, paranormal romantic comedy, Zomopolis, and a new western romance entitled, The Fire In Their Hearts co-authored with R.S. Meger. In addition the near future suspense novel, The Last Serial Killer by R.G. Crossley was recently released.

He has sold several short stories that have appeared in anthologies from Pocket Books, St. Matins Press, at Smashwords, Amazon, and other e-retail sites.

With his wife, romance author R.S. Meger, he owns and operates a small press publishing company, 53rd Street Publishing. The company began in April 2011 and now has over one hundred e-book titles and a number of print titles, with more planned in 2012 and 2013.

He is a member of SF Canada and the Greater Vancouver Chapter of Romance Writers of America. He is also an alumni of the Oregon Coast Professional Fiction Writers Master Class taught by award winning author/editors, Kristine Katherine Rusch and Dean Wesley Smith.

To find a complete listing of his work check out his website http://www.rghart.com,
http://russstory.blogspot.com.
Razor's blog can be found at
http://razorandedge.blogspot.com
Feel free to contact him on Facebook or Twitter. He loves to hear from readers

Other books by the Author

Titles as R.G. Crossley

Short Stories

Razor and Edge Mysteries
The Kidnapping of Billy Buttons
String of Pearls
Death by Clown
Beggin' For Murder
Ragged Ice
The Grand Central Mystery

Non-Series Mysteries
A Day Without Sunshine
Mirror Image
Dangerous Waters
Cape Disappointment
Boomerang
The Watcher of Wayburn Street
The Apprentice
Drip!
A Beautiful Friendship and The Parrot of Doom
Robine's Diary
The Christmas Club
Loose Ends
Skullduggery
Splatter Pattern
It Takes Two

Anthologies
The Adventures of Razor and Edge:
Five Tales From The Quirky Detective Team

Novels
A Bad Case of Loyalty
The Last Serial Killer

Titles as Russ Crossley

Novels
Attack of the Lushites

Short Stories
Countdown
Shoeless Moe
Round Up At The Burger Bar:
The Story of Trixie Pug, Parts 1, 2, 3, 4, 5, 6
Five Minutes
Blossom Queen, Barbarian
The Secret
The Family Line
End of the Flies
With Death You Get the Eggroll
The Penguin Sleeps With The Fishes
Only The Worthy
Hero For A Day
End of Empire
Strange Bedfellows
Big Business
A Perfect Crime
The Wise Guy and The Pirates

Titles as R.G. Hart

Short Stories
Tikka's Big Day
"My Partner the Zombie" —
Hungry For Your Love Anthology
(St. Martin's Press)
Big Hairy Deal
One Red Shoe
A Bad Day in Lunden Texas
Hook Island
Grind Manor

Novels
Bachelorette: Zombie Edition
(from Champagne Books)
Antique Virgin
The Fire In Their Hearts
with R.S. Meger (coming soon from
Champagne Books)
Zomopolis

www.ingramcontent.com/pod-product-compliance
Lightning Source LLC
Chambersburg PA
CBHW020308150626
46552CB00022B/2168